Cici #3
A Fairy's Tale

ᕼA PERFECT VIEWᕼ

Written by
Cori Doerrfeld

Illustrated by
Tyler Page and
Cori Doerrfeld

GRAPHIC UNIVERSE™ • MINNEAPOLIS

Graphic Universe™ is a trademark of Lerner Publishing Group, Inc.

Graphic Universe™
A division of Lerner Publishing Group, Inc.
241 First Avenue North
Minneapolis, MN 55401 USA

For reading levels and more information, look up this title at www.lernerbooks.com.

Main body text set in CCDaveGibbonsLower 10/11.
Typeface provided by ComicCraft.

Library of Congress Cataloging-in-Publication Data

Names: Doerrfeld, Cori, author, illustrator. | Page, Tyler, 1976– illustrator.
Title: A Perfect View / written by Cori Doerrfeld ; illustrated by Tyler Page and Cori Doerrfeld.
Description: Minneapolis : Graphic Universe, [2017] | Series: Cici: a fairy's tale ; 3 | Summary: "While camping, Cici finds out that she experiences nature differently as a fairy, which turns all her plans upside-down" –Provided by publisher.
Identifiers: LCCN 2015044432 | ISBN 9781467761543 (lb : alk. paper) | ISBN 9781512430684 (pbk.) | ISBN 9781512427004 (eb pdf)
Subjects: LCSH: Graphic novels. | CYAC: Graphic novels. | Fairies–Fiction. | Magic–Fiction. | Camping–Fiction. | Hispanic Americans–Fiction.
Classification: LCC PZ7.7.D634 Pe 2017 | DDC 741.5/973–dc23

LC record available at https://lccn.loc.gov/2015044432

Manufactured in the United States of America
1-37129-18117-4/13/2016

For Erin

—C.D.

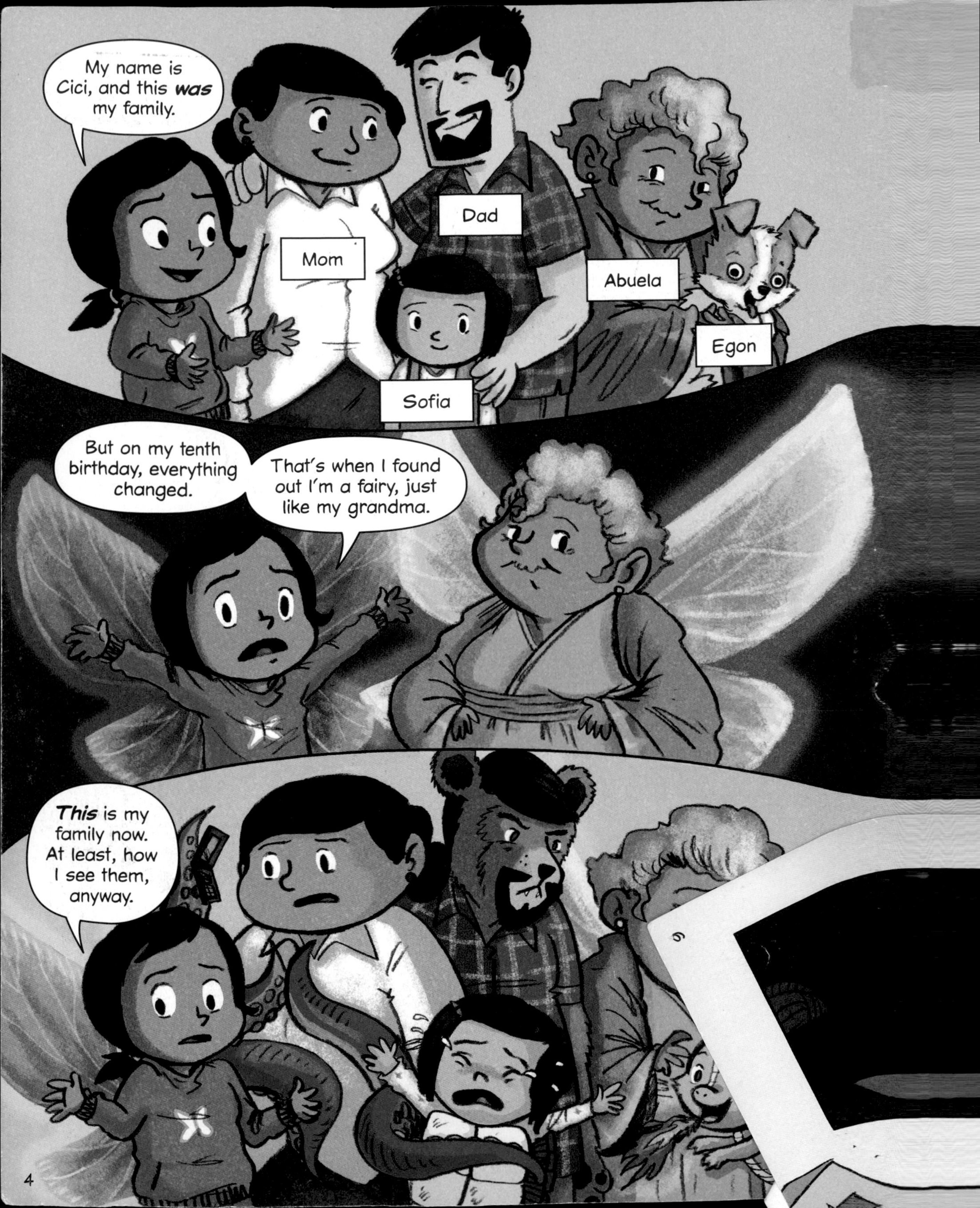
My name is Cici, and this ***was*** my family.
Mom
Dad
Abuela
Egon
Sofia
But on my tenth birthday, everything changed.
That's when I found out I'm a fairy, just like my grandma.
This is my family now. At least, how I see them, anyway.

For Erin

—C.D.

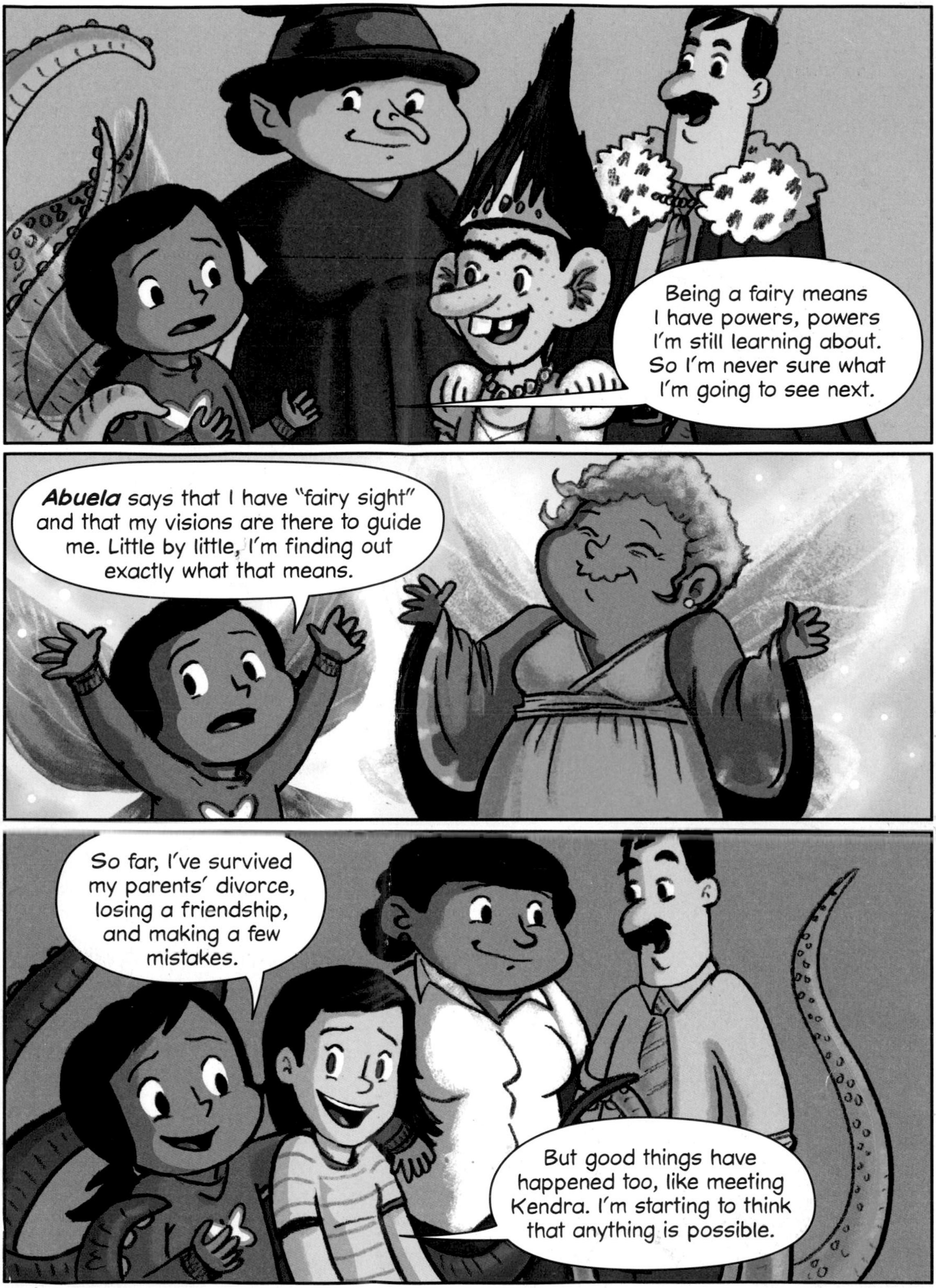
Being a fairy means I have powers, powers I'm still learning about. So I'm never sure what I'm going to see next.
Abuela says that I have "fairy sight" and that my visions are there to guide me. Little by little, I'm finding out exactly what that means.
So far, I've survived my parents' divorce, losing a friendship, and making a few mistakes.
But good things have happened too, like meeting Kendra. I'm starting to think that anything is possible.

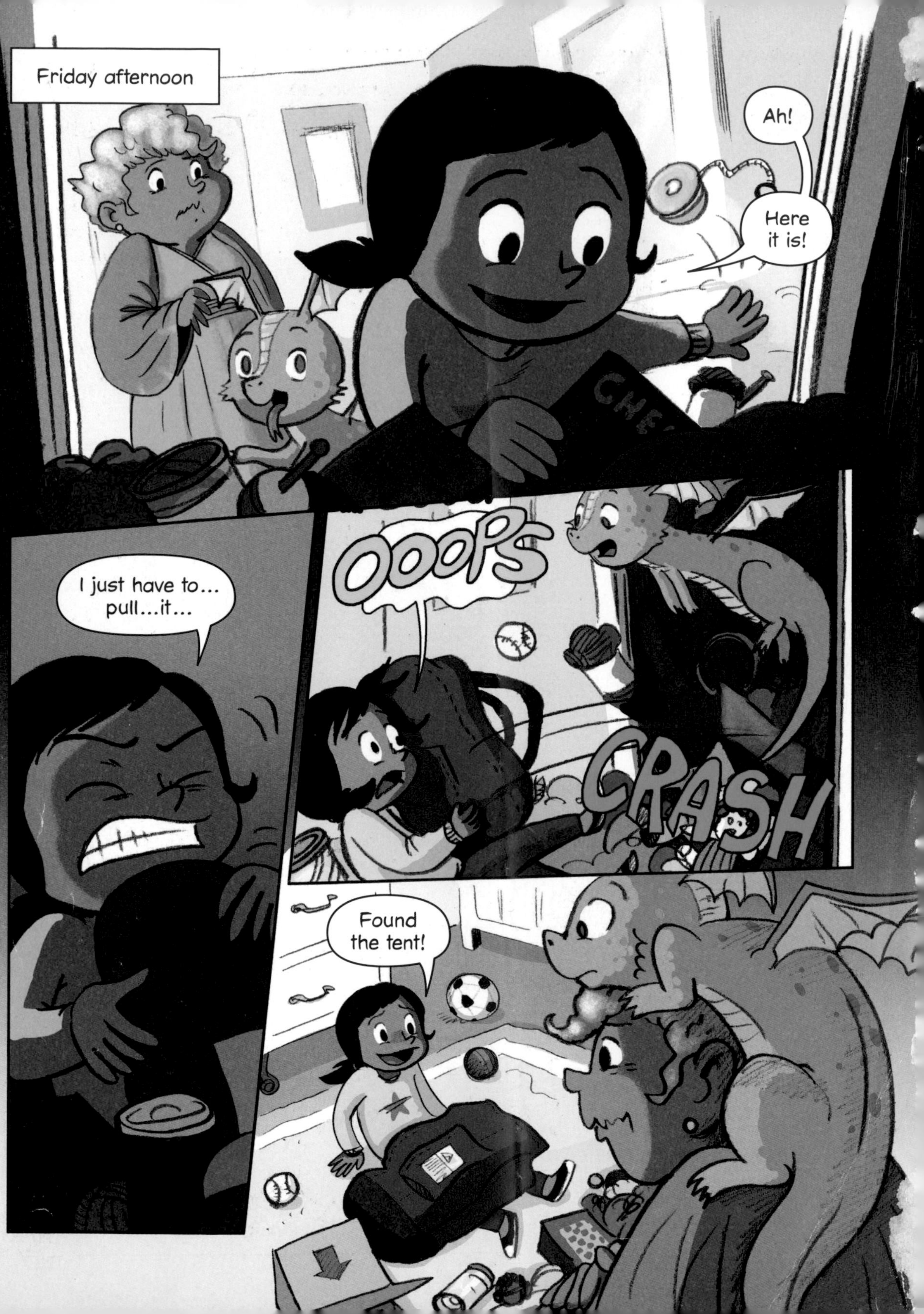
Friday afternoon
Ah!
Here it is!
I just have to... pull...it...
OOOPS
CRASH
Found the tent!

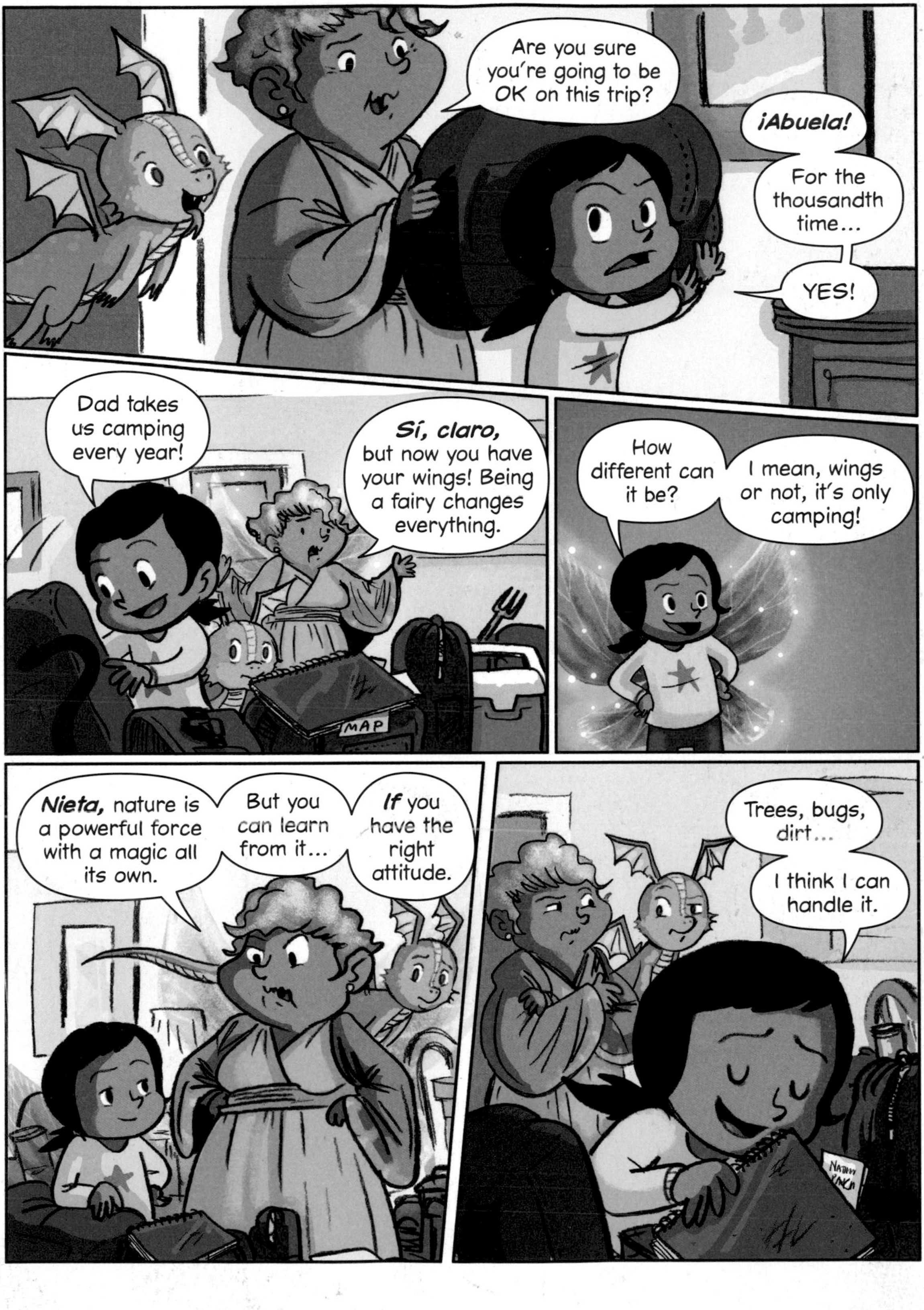
Are you sure you're going to be OK on this trip?
¡Abuela!
For the thousandth time...
YES!
Dad takes us camping every year!
Sí, claro, but now you have your wings! Being a fairy changes everything.
MAP
How different can it be?
I mean, wings or not, it's only camping!
Nieta, nature is a powerful force with a magic all its own.
But you can learn from it...
If you have the right attitude.
Trees, bugs, dirt...
I think I can handle it.

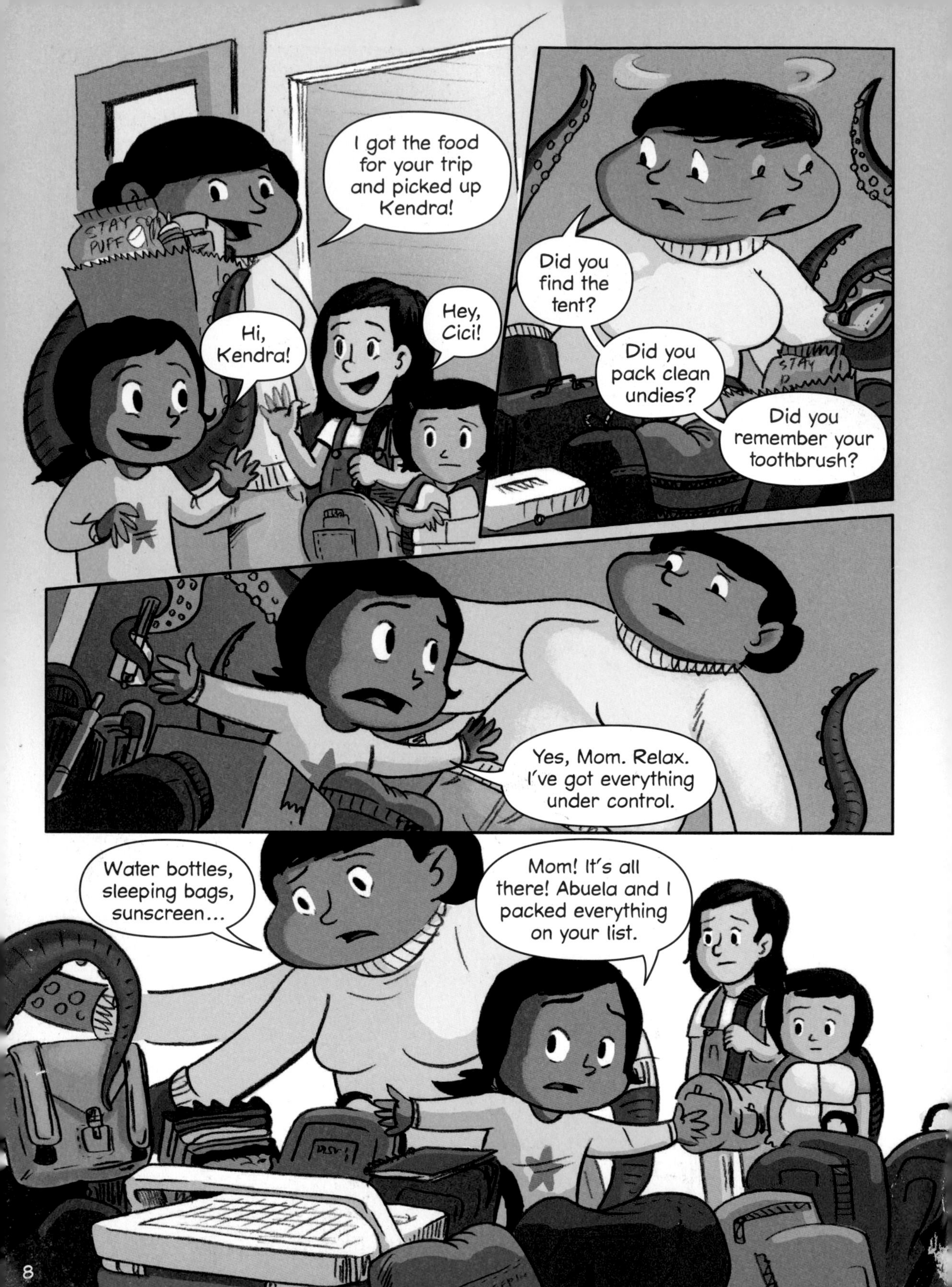
STAY PUFF
I got the food for your trip and picked up Kendra!
Hi, Kendra!
Hey, Cici!
Did you find the tent?
Did you pack clean undies?
Did you remember your toothbrush?
Yes, Mom. Relax. I've got everything under control.
Water bottles, sleeping bags, sunscreen...
Mom! It's all there! Abuela and I packed everything on your list.

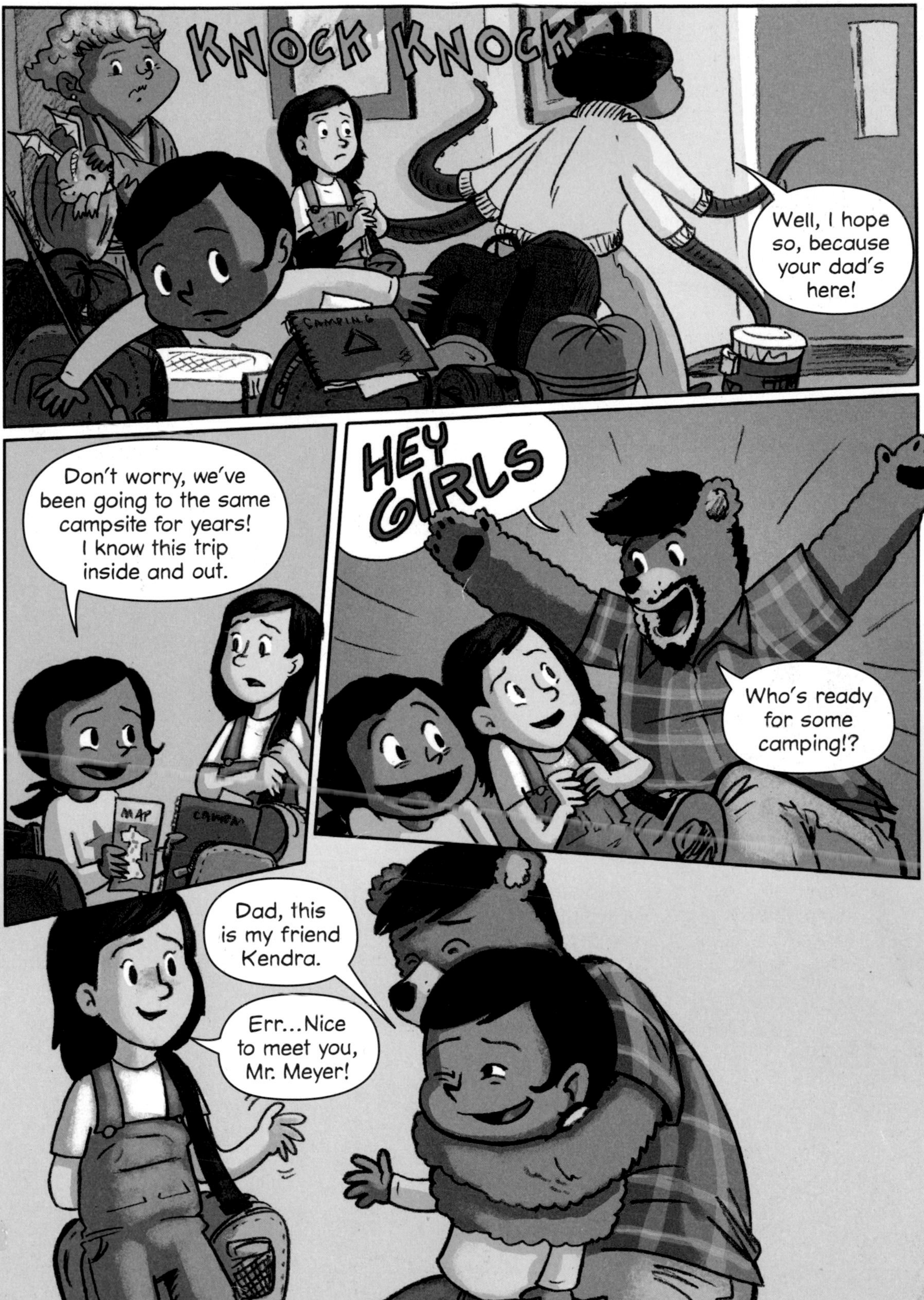
KNOCK KNOCK
Well, I hope so, because your dad's here!
Don't worry, we've been going to the same campsite for years! I know this trip inside and out.
HEY GIRLS
Who's ready for some camping!?
Dad, this is my friend Kendra.
Err...Nice to meet you, Mr. Meyer!

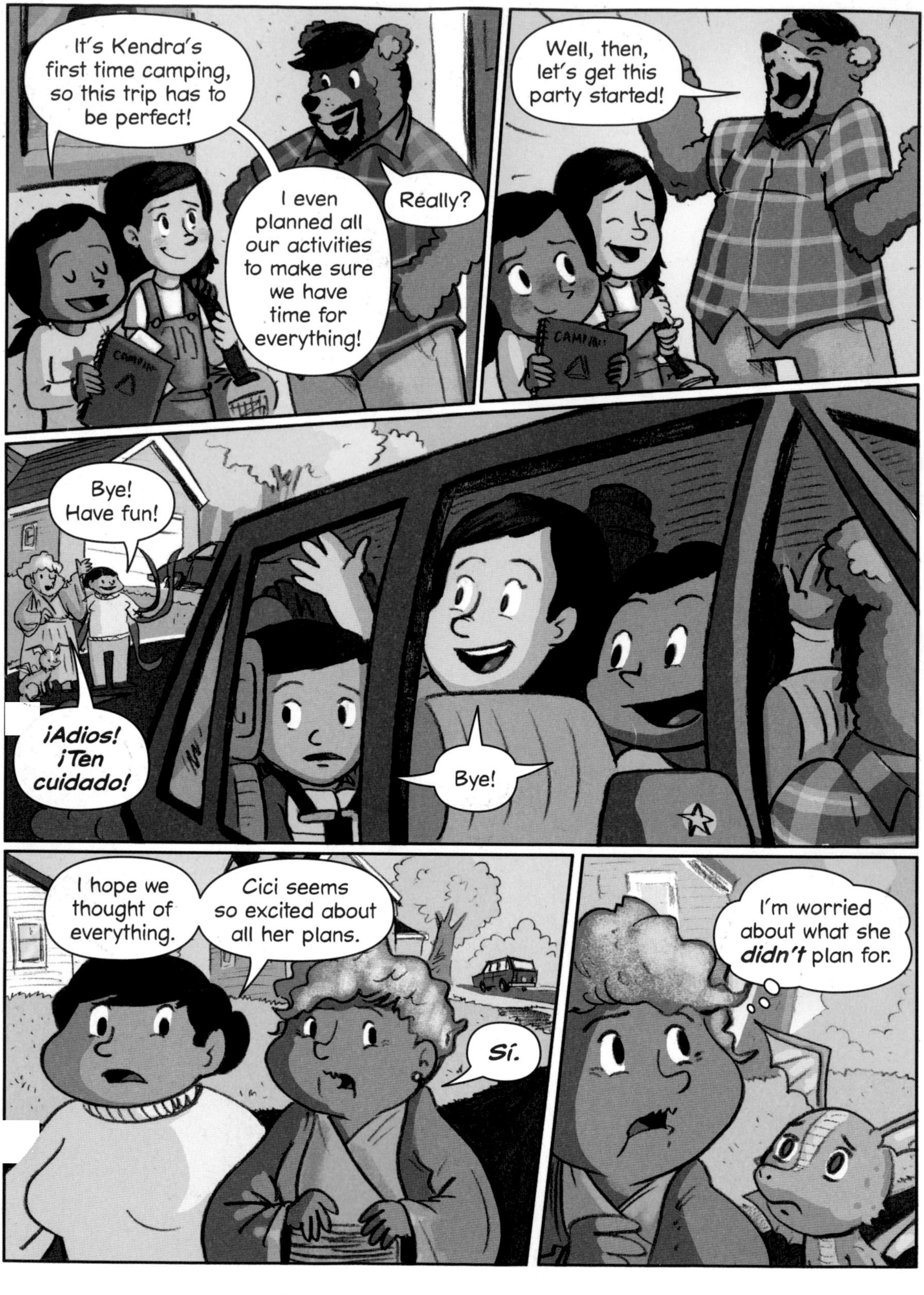

It's Kendra's first time camping, so this trip has to be perfect!
Really?
I even planned all our activities to make sure we have time for everything!
Well, then, let's get this party started!
Bye! Have fun!
¡Adios! ¡Ten cuidado!
Bye!
I hope we thought of everything.
Cici seems so excited about all her plans.
Sí.
I'm worried about what she *didn't* plan for.

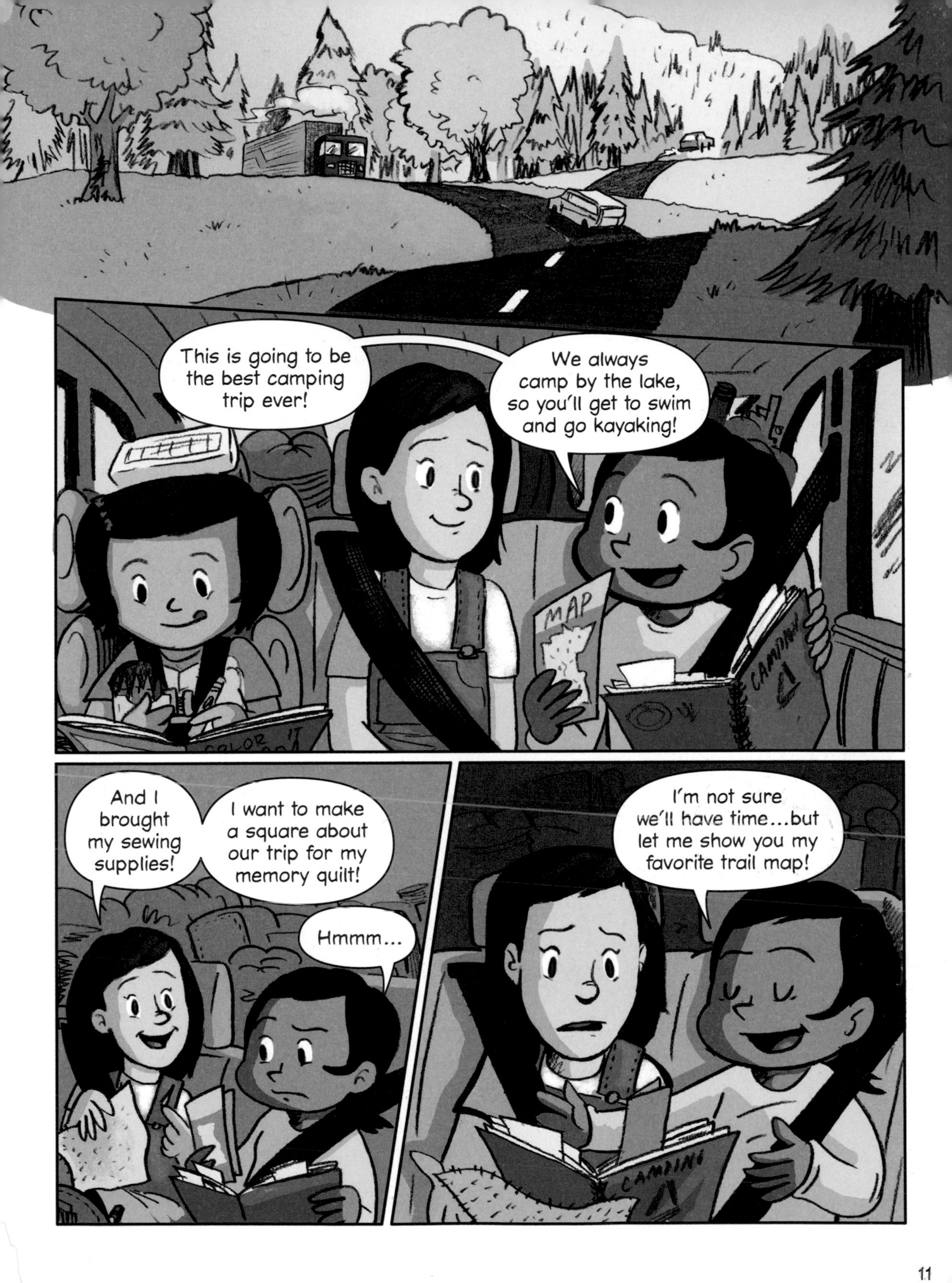
This is going to be the best camping trip ever!
We always camp by the lake, so you'll get to swim and go kayaking!
MAP
And I brought my sewing supplies!
I want to make a square about our trip for my memory quilt!
Hmmm...
I'm not sure we'll have time...but let me show you my favorite trail map!
CAMPING

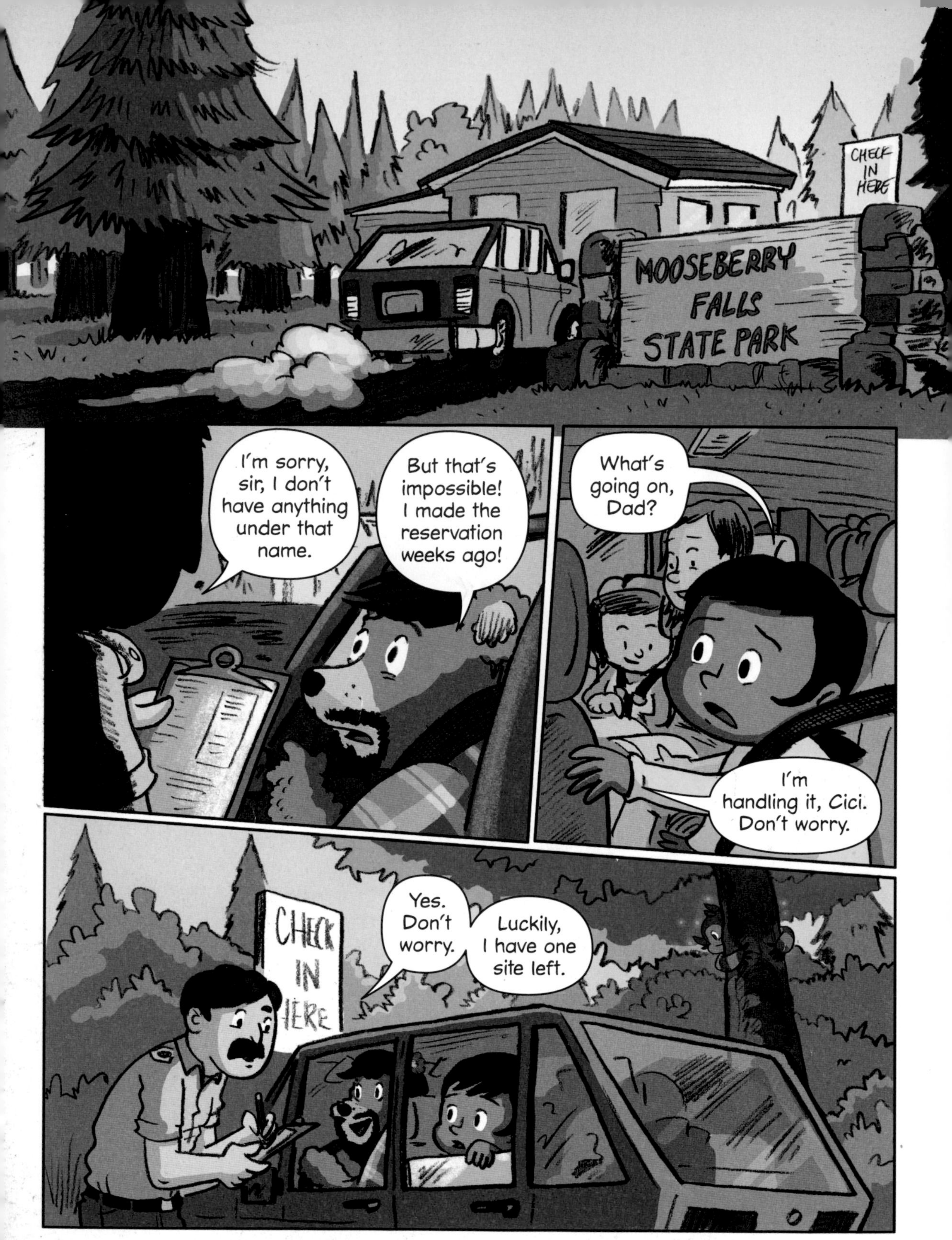
CHECK IN HERE
MOOSEBERRY FALLS STATE PARK
I'm sorry, sir, I don't have anything under that name.
But that's impossible! I made the reservation weeks ago!
What's going on, Dad?
I'm handling it, Cici. Don't worry.
CHECK IN HERE
Yes. Don't worry.
Luckily, I have one site left.

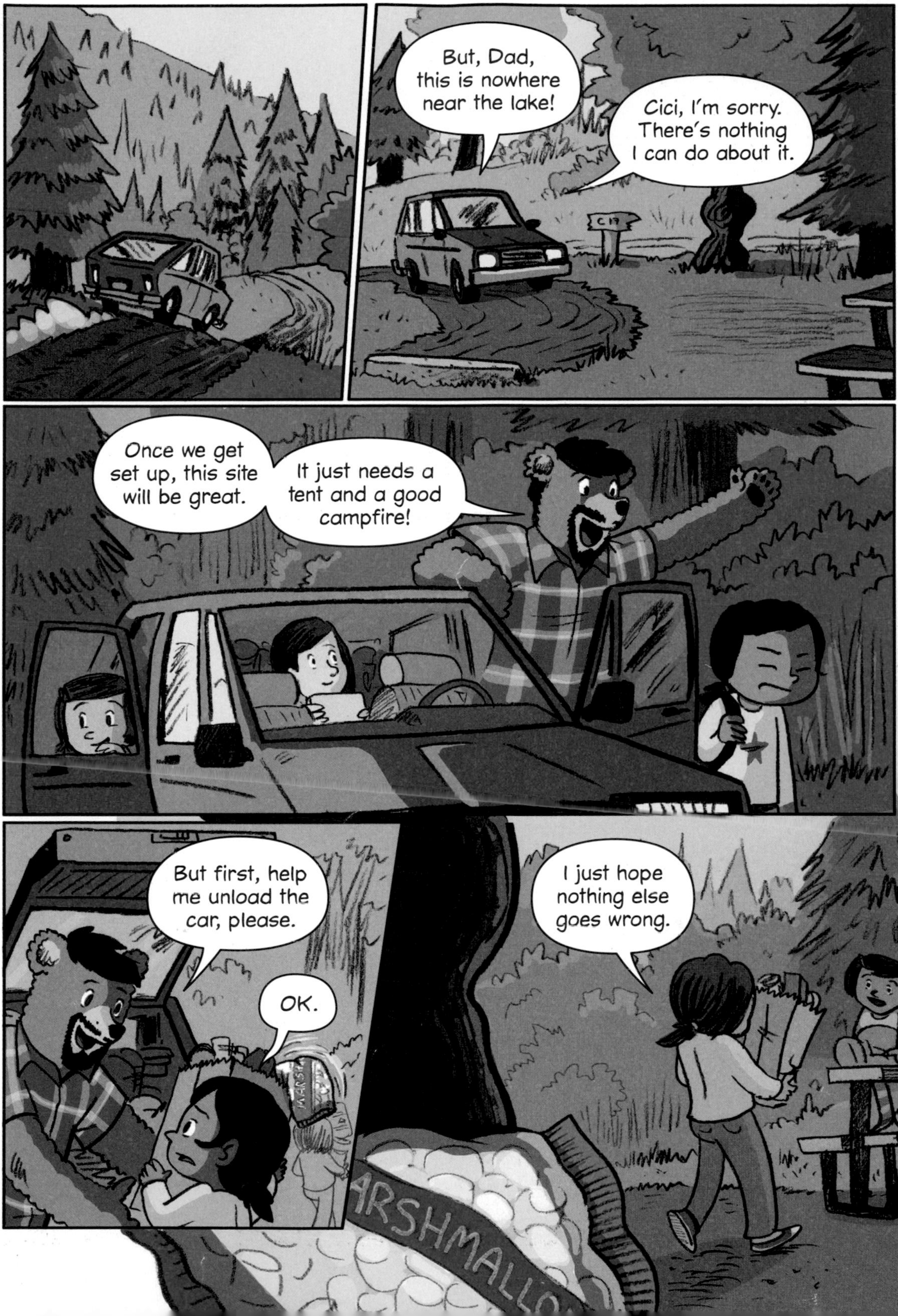
But, Dad, this is nowhere near the lake!
Cici, I'm sorry. There's nothing I can do about it.
Once we get set up, this site will be great.
It just needs a tent and a good campfire!
But first, help me unload the car, please.
OK.
I just hope nothing else goes wrong.
ARSHMALLO

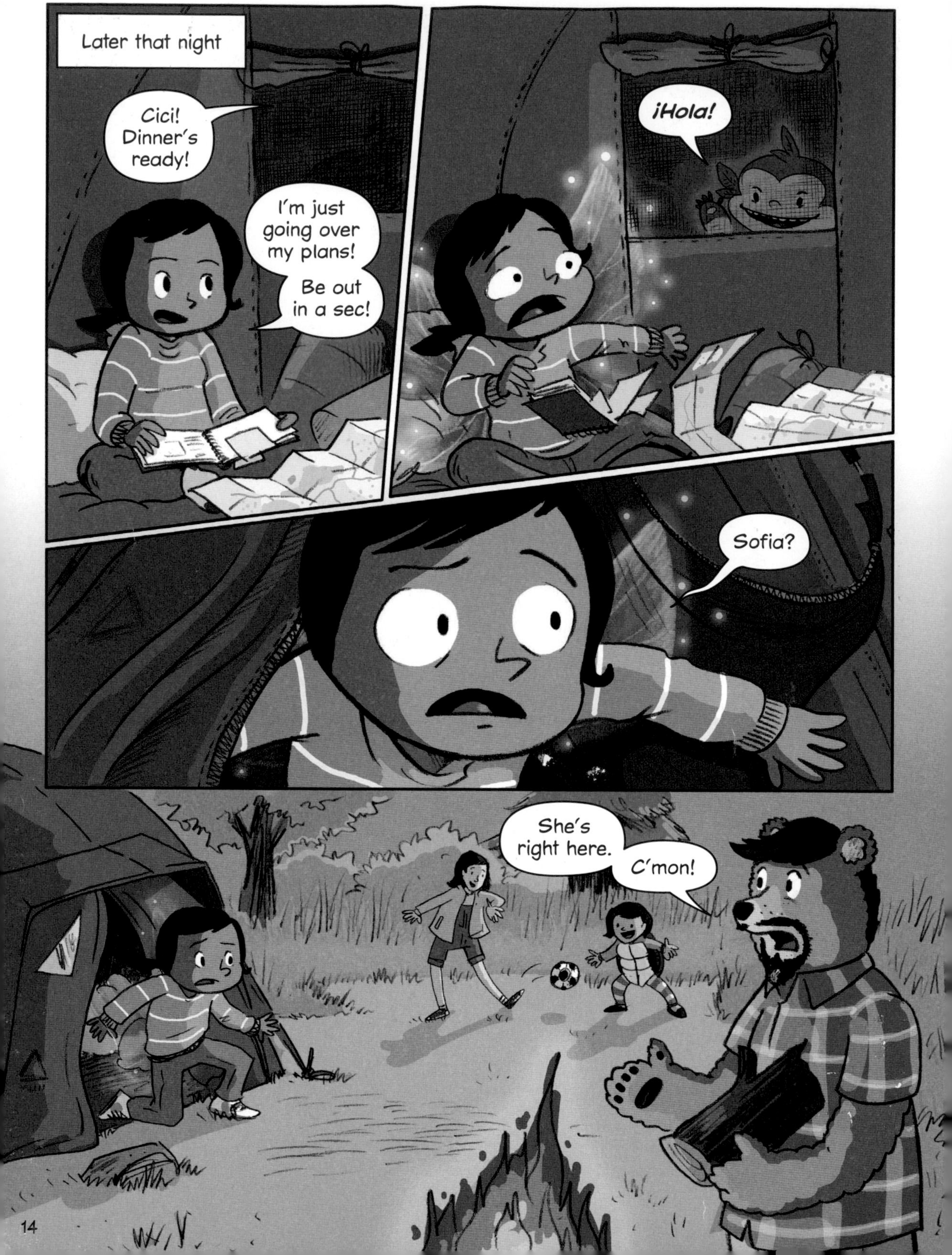
Later that night
Cici! Dinner's ready!
I'm just going over my plans!
Be out in a sec!
¡Hola!
Sofia?
She's right here.
C'mon!

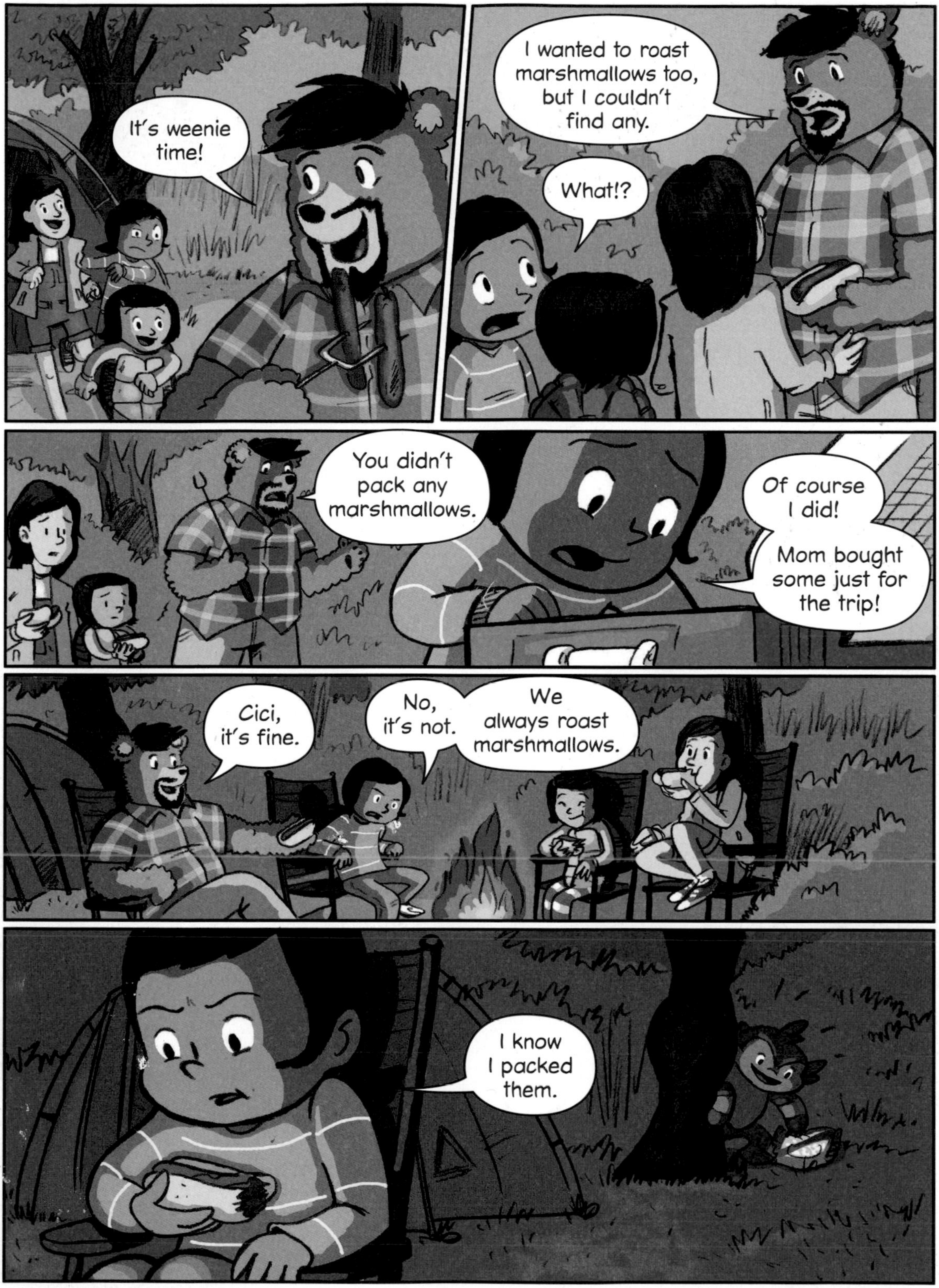
It's weenie time!
I wanted to roast marshmallows too, but I couldn't find any.
What!?
You didn't pack any marshmallows.
Of course I did!
Mom bought some just for the trip!
Cici, it's fine.
No, it's not.
We always roast marshmallows.
I know I packed them.

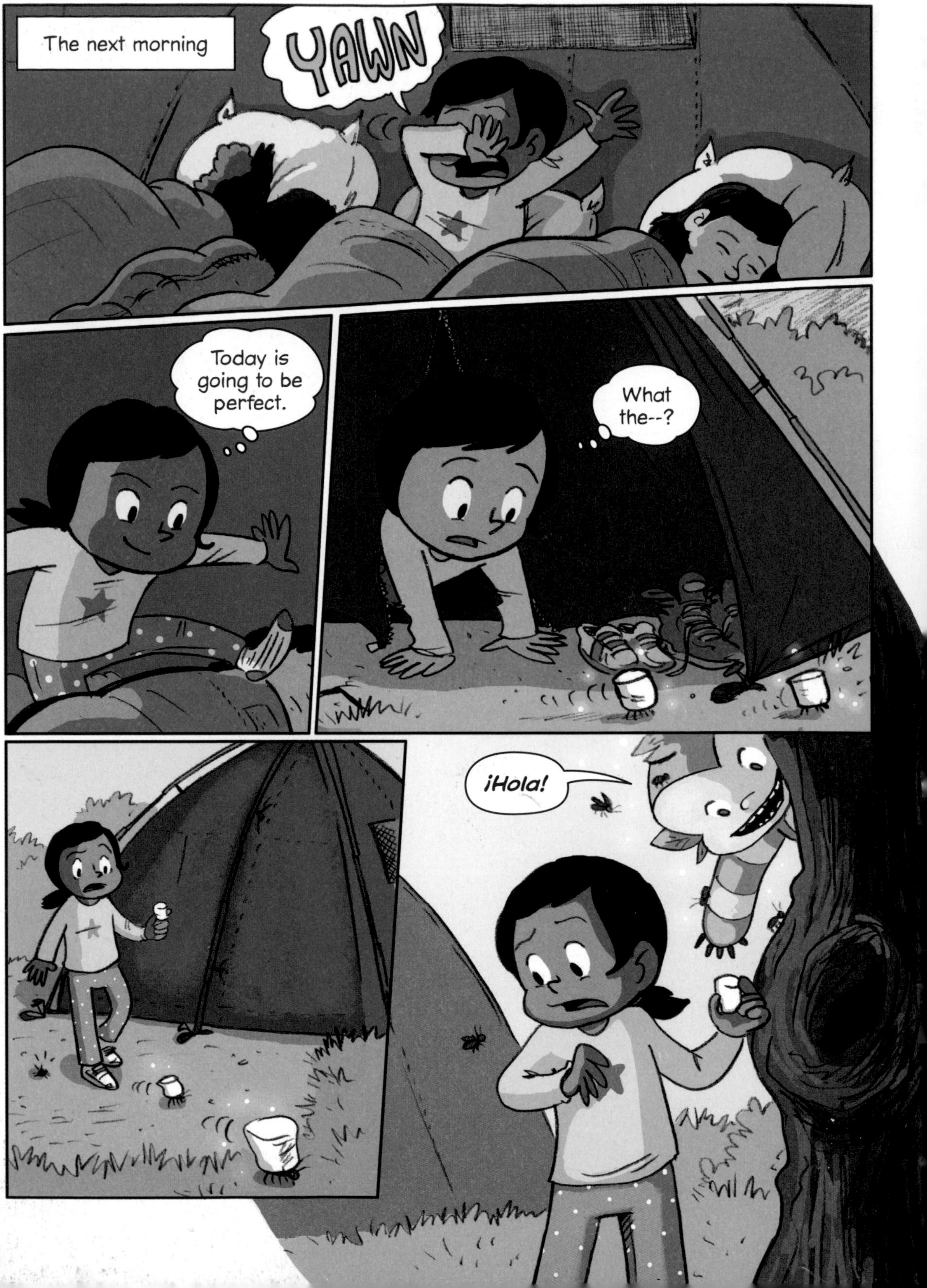
The next morning
YAWN
Today is going to be perfect.
What the--?
¡Hola!

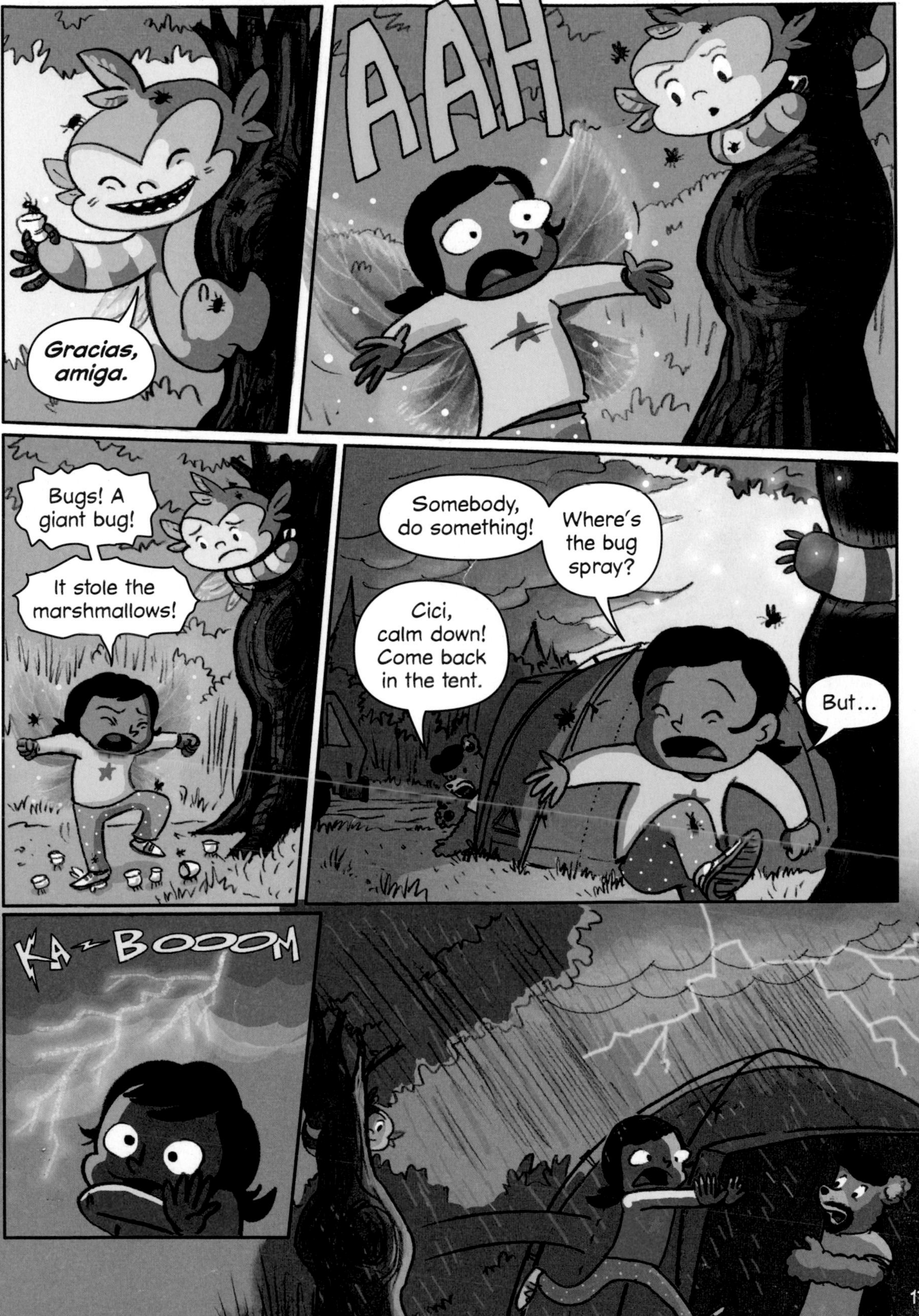
Gracias, amiga.
AAH
Bugs! A giant bug!
It stole the marshmallows!
Somebody, do something!
Where's the bug spray?
Cici, calm down! Come back in the tent.
But...
KA-BOOOOM

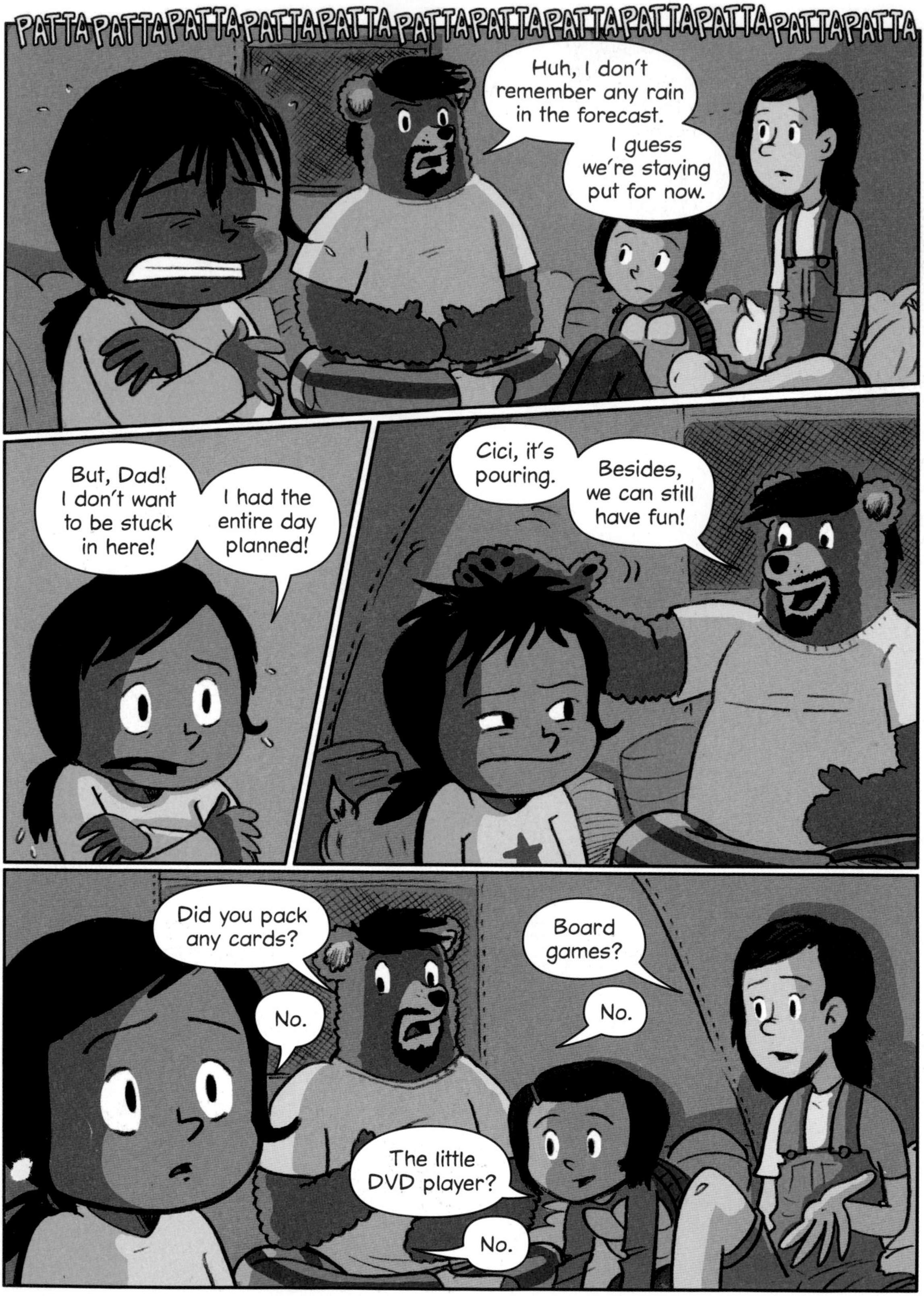
PATTAPATTAPATTAPATTAPATTAPATTAPATTAPATTAPATTAPATTAPATTAPATTA
Huh, I don't remember any rain in the forecast.
I guess we're staying put for now.
But, Dad! I don't want to be stuck in here!
I had the entire day planned!
Cici, it's pouring.
Besides, we can still have fun!
Did you pack any cards?
No.
Board games?
No.
The little DVD player?
No.

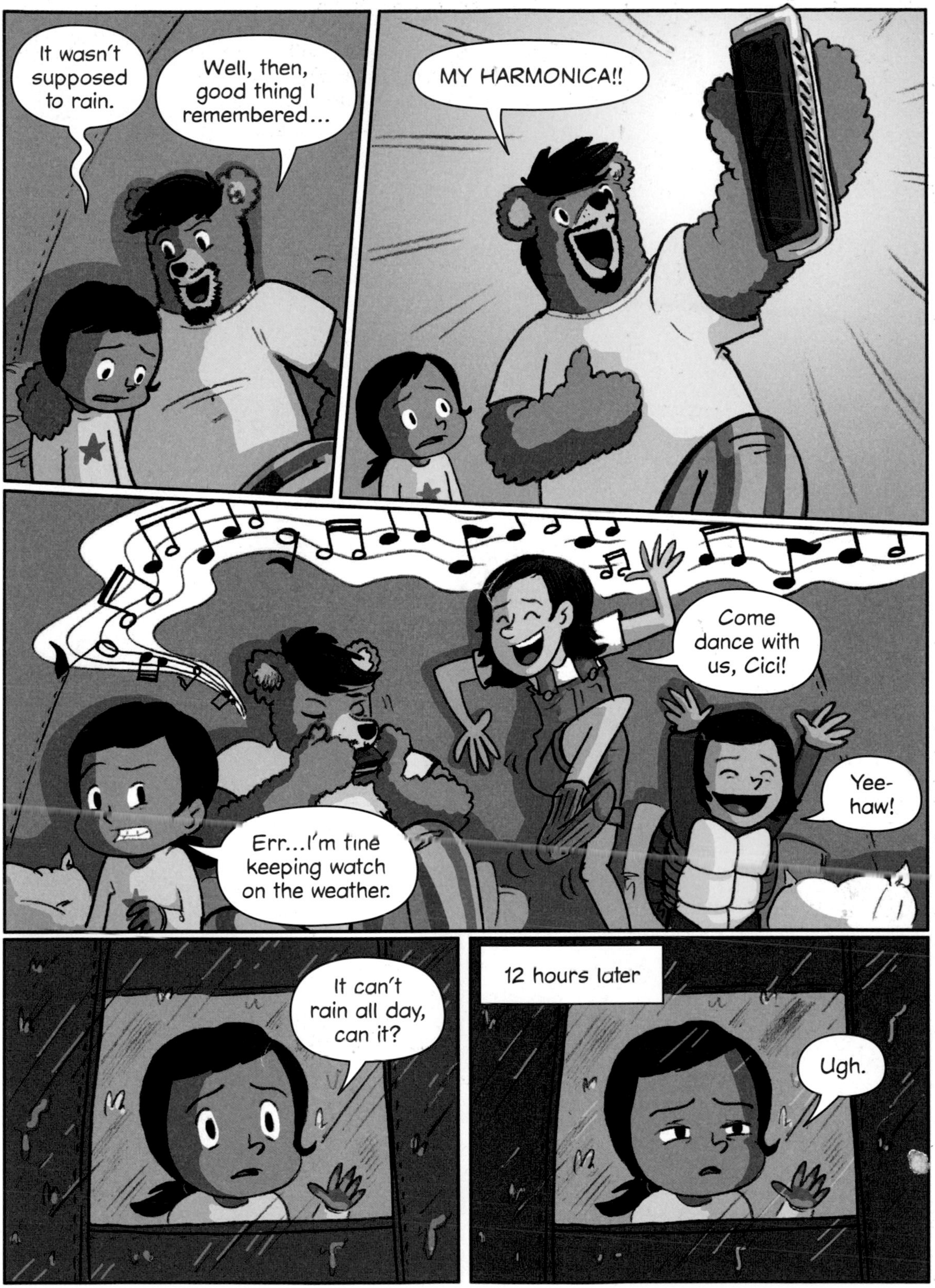
It wasn't supposed to rain.
Well, then, good thing I remembered...
MY HARMONICA!!
Come dance with us, Cici!
Yee-haw!
Err...I'm fine keeping watch on the weather.
It can't rain all day, can it?
12 hours later
Ugh.

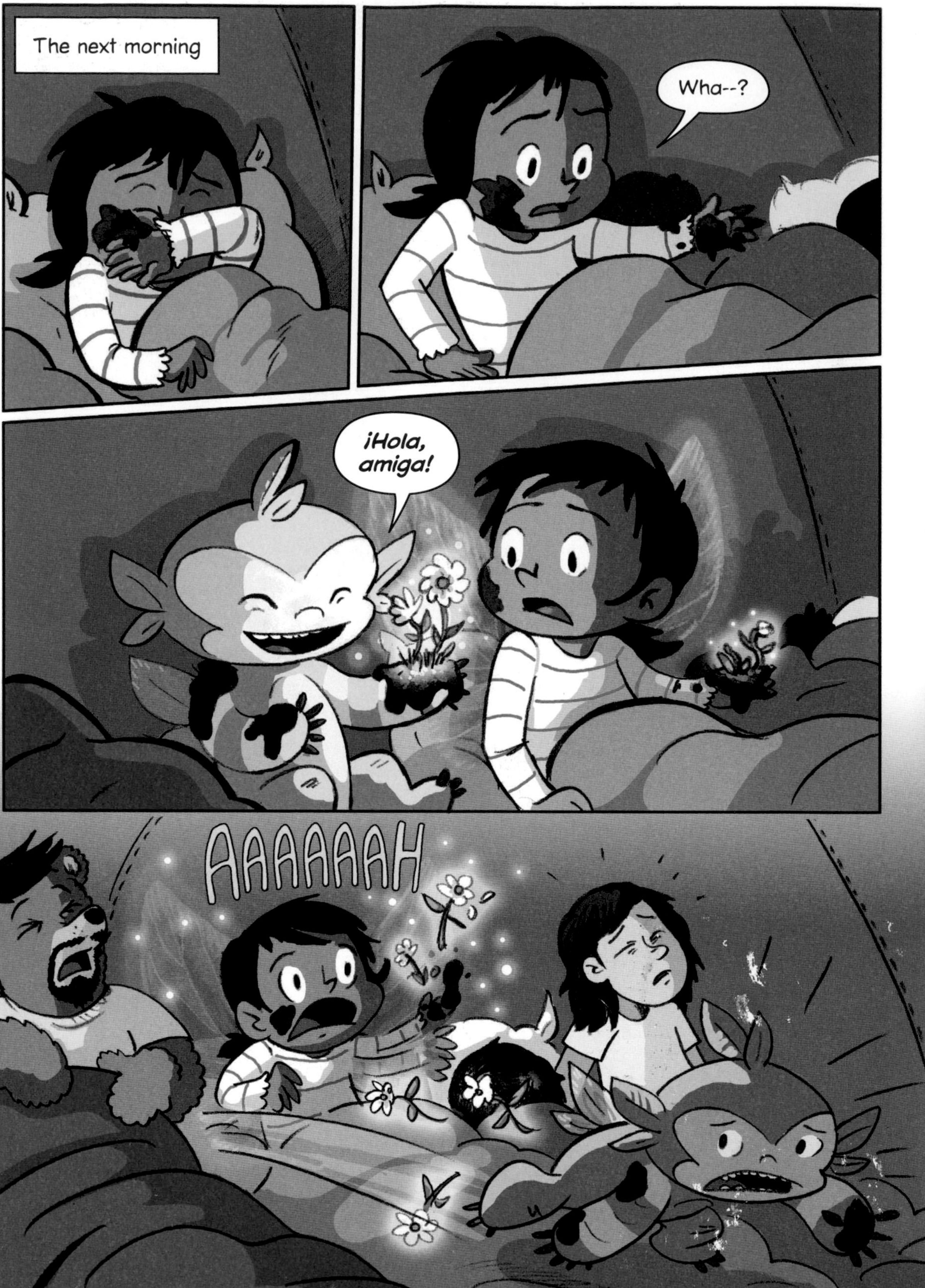
The next morning
Wha--?
¡Hola, amiga!
AAAAAAH

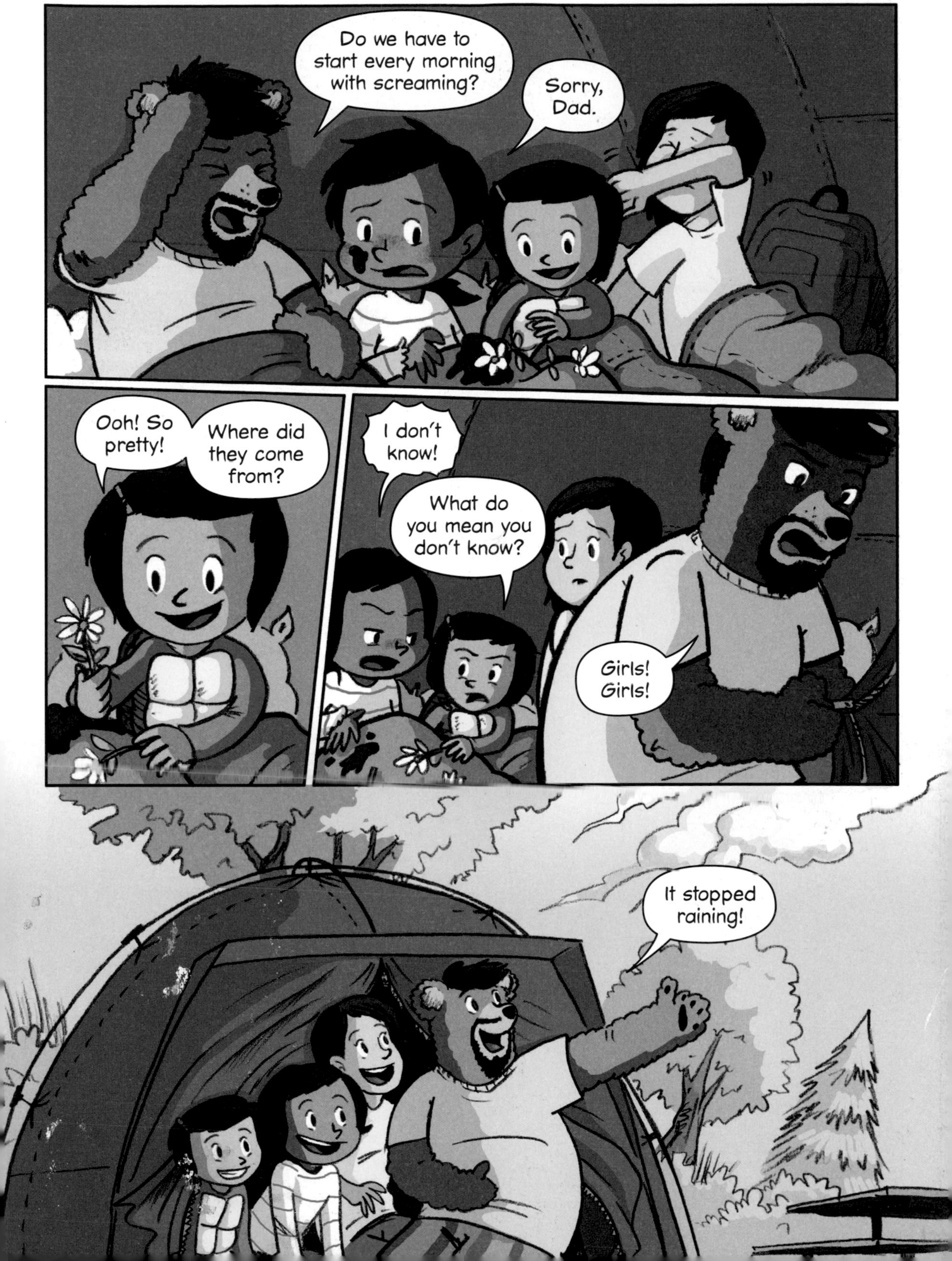
Do we have to start every morning with screaming?
Sorry, Dad.
Ooh! So pretty!
Where did they come from?
I don't know!
What do you mean you don't know?
Girls! Girls!
It stopped raining!

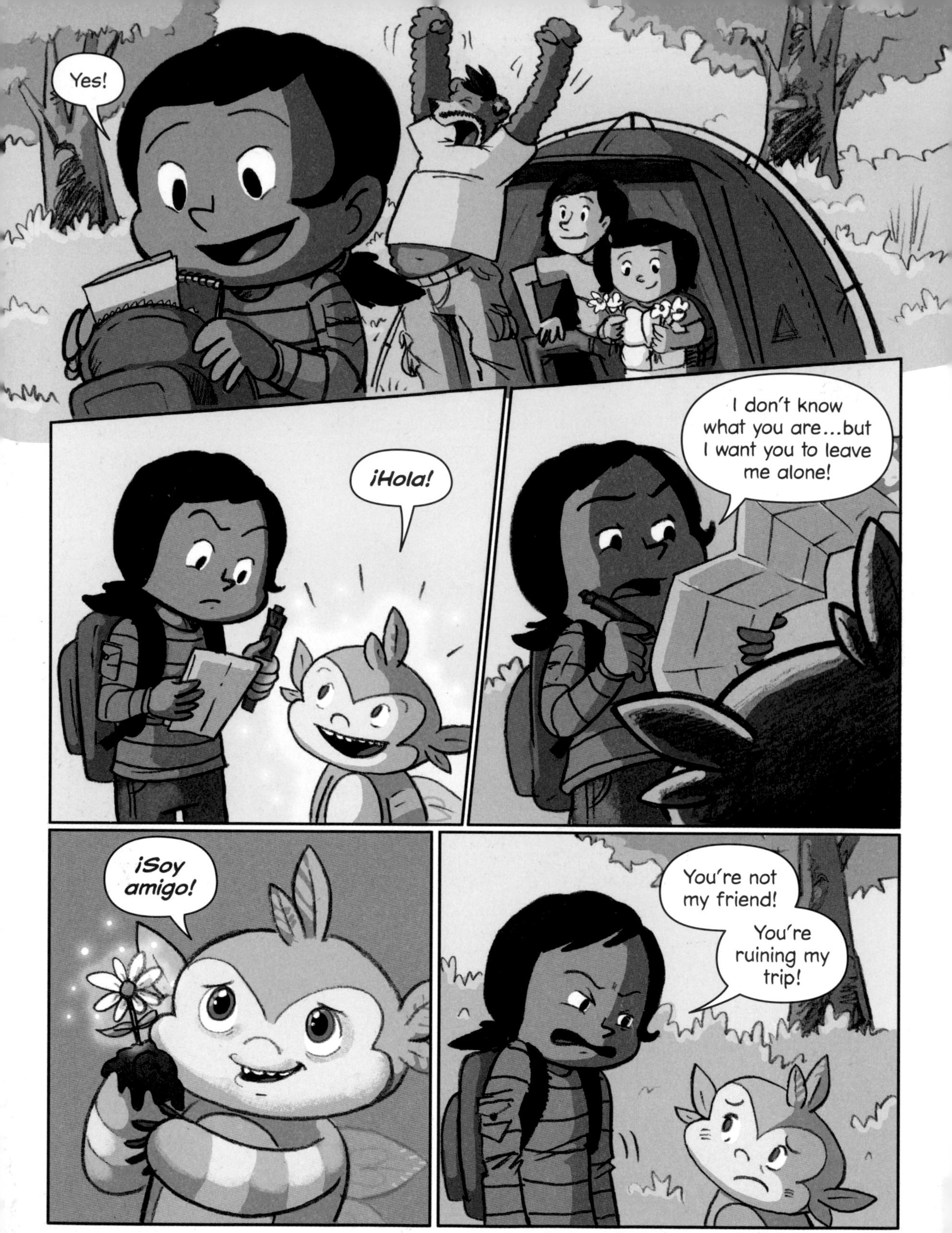
Yes!
¡Hola!
I don't know what you are...but I want you to leave me alone!
¡Soy amigo!
You're not my friend!
You're ruining my trip!

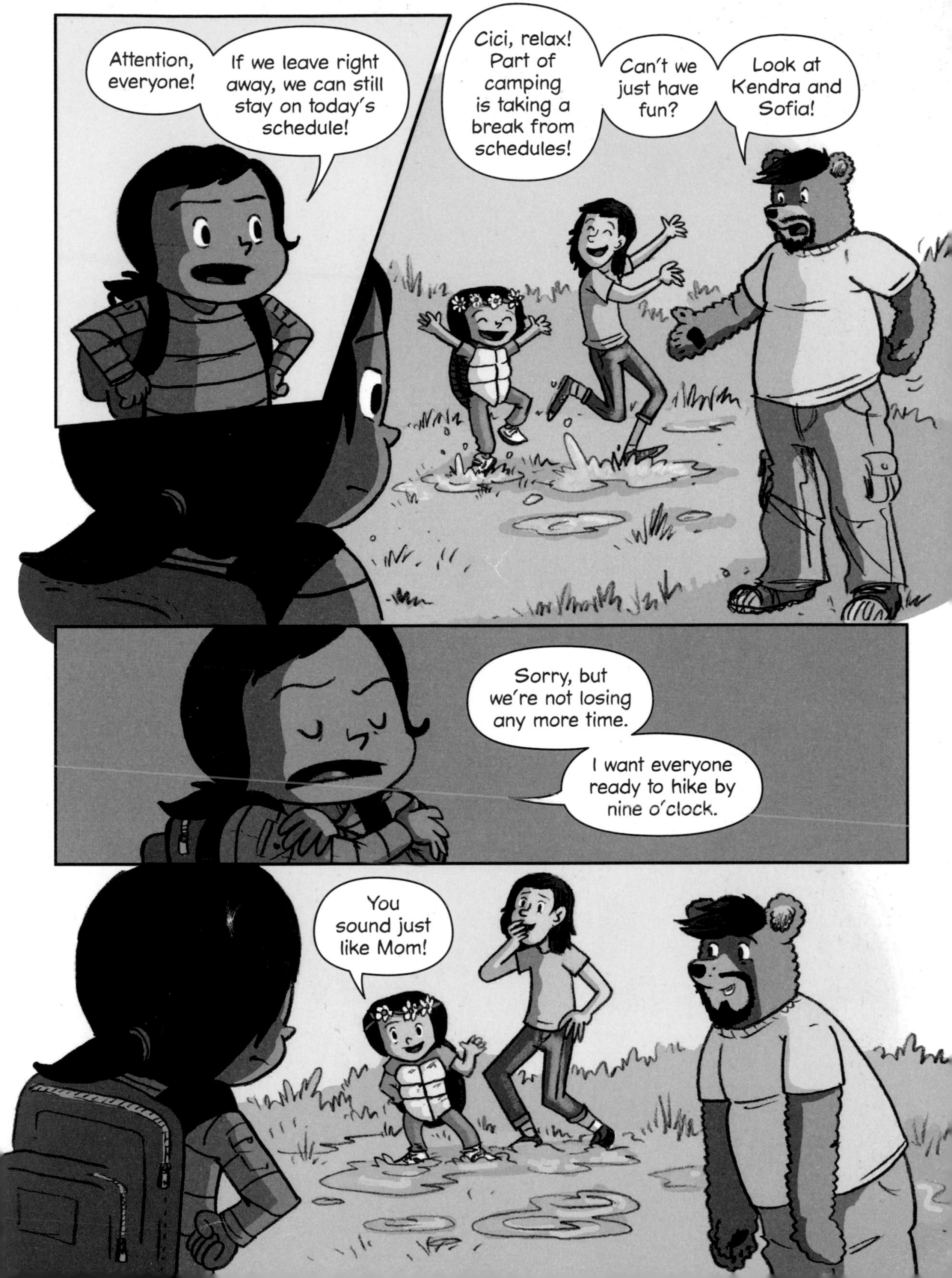
Attention, everyone!
If we leave right away, we can still stay on today's schedule!
Cici, relax! Part of camping is taking a break from schedules!
Can't we just have fun?
Look at Kendra and Sofia!
Sorry, but we're not losing any more time.
I want everyone ready to hike by nine o'clock.
You sound just like Mom!

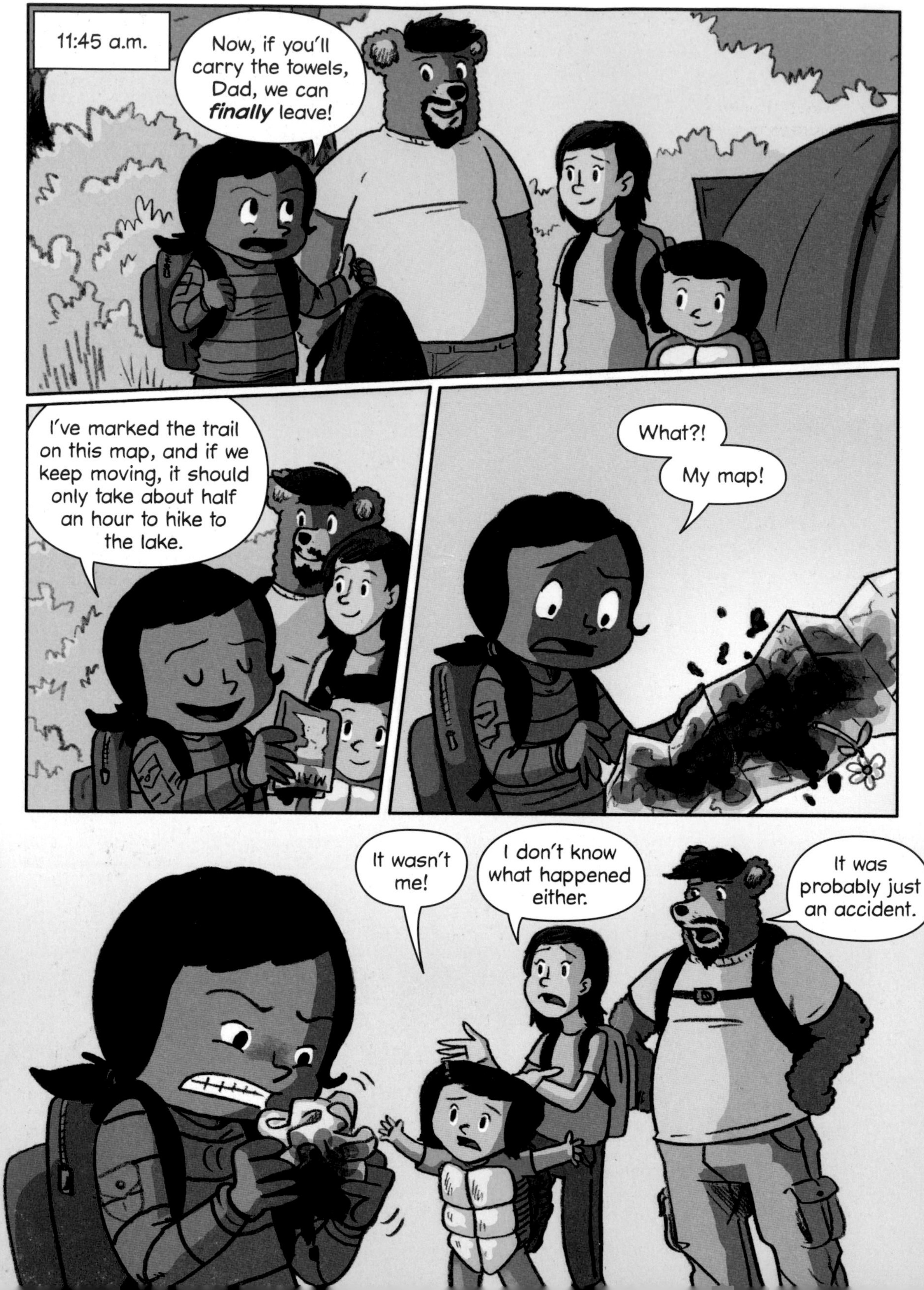
11:45 a.m.
Now, if you'll carry the towels, Dad, we can *finally* leave!
I've marked the trail on this map, and if we keep moving, it should only take about half an hour to hike to the lake.
What?!
My map!
It wasn't me!
I don't know what happened either.
It was probably just an accident.

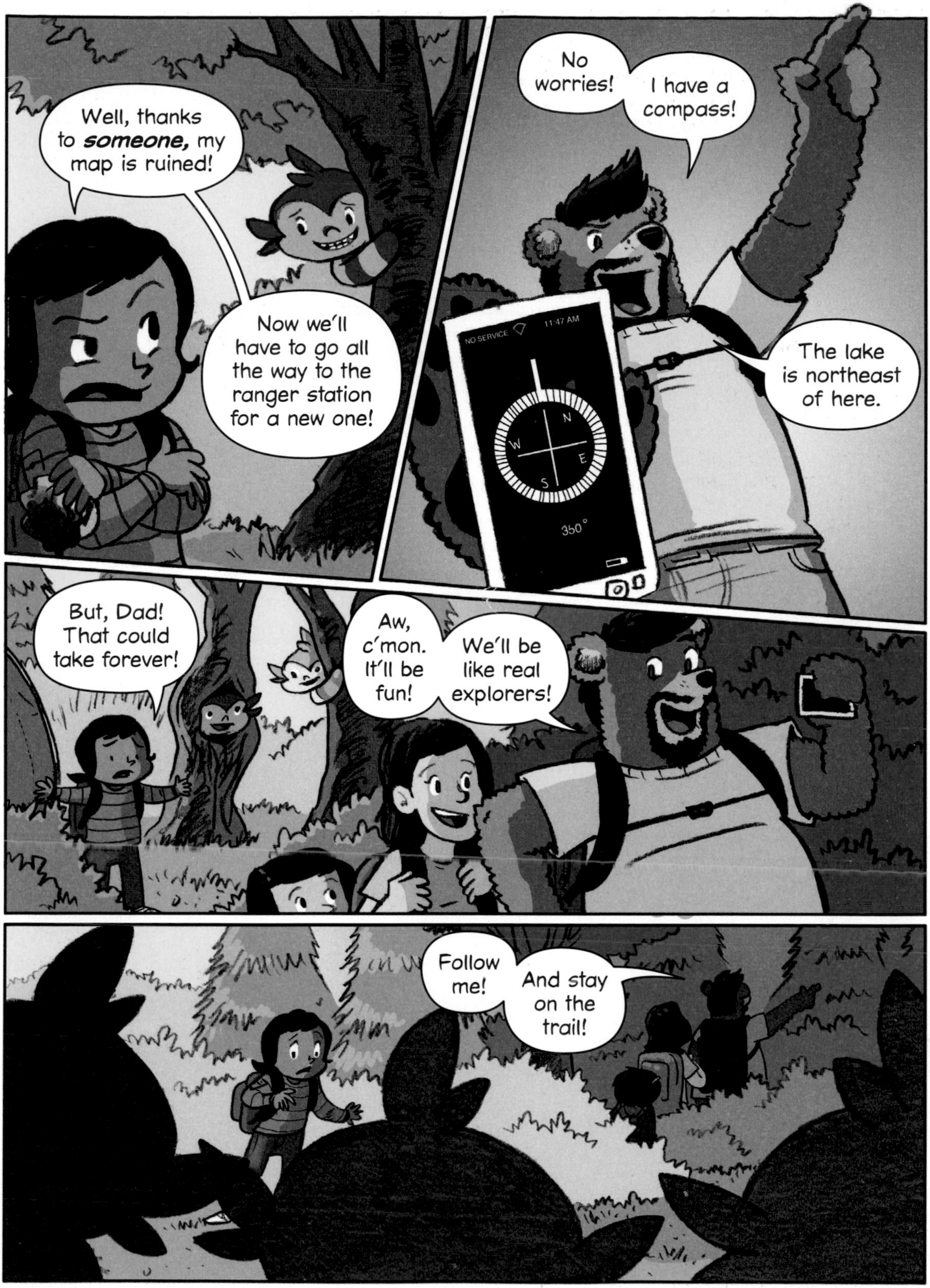

Well, thanks to ***someone,*** my map is ruined!
Now we'll have to go all the way to the ranger station for a new one!
No worries!
I have a compass!
NO SERVICE
11:47 AM
N
W
E
S
360°
The lake is northeast of here.
But, Dad! That could take forever!
Aw, c'mon. It'll be fun!
We'll be like real explorers!
Follow me!
And stay on the trail!

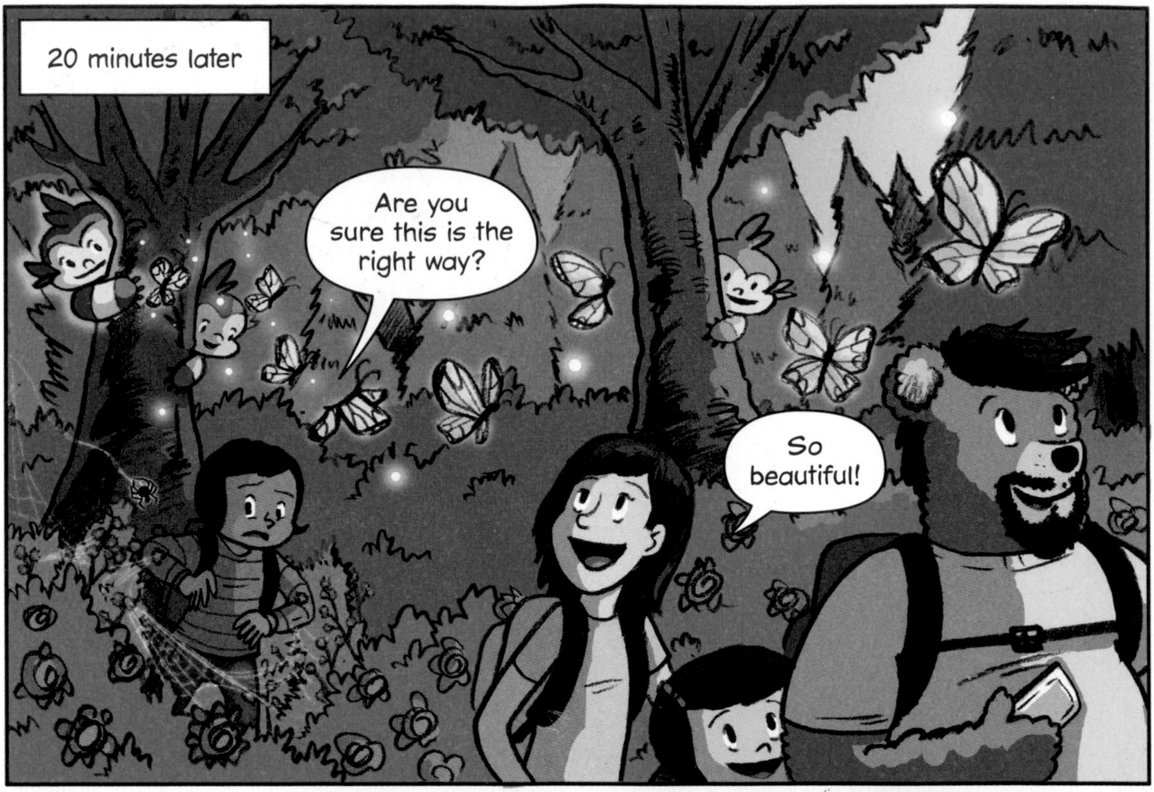
20 minutes later
Are you sure this is the right way?
So beautiful!

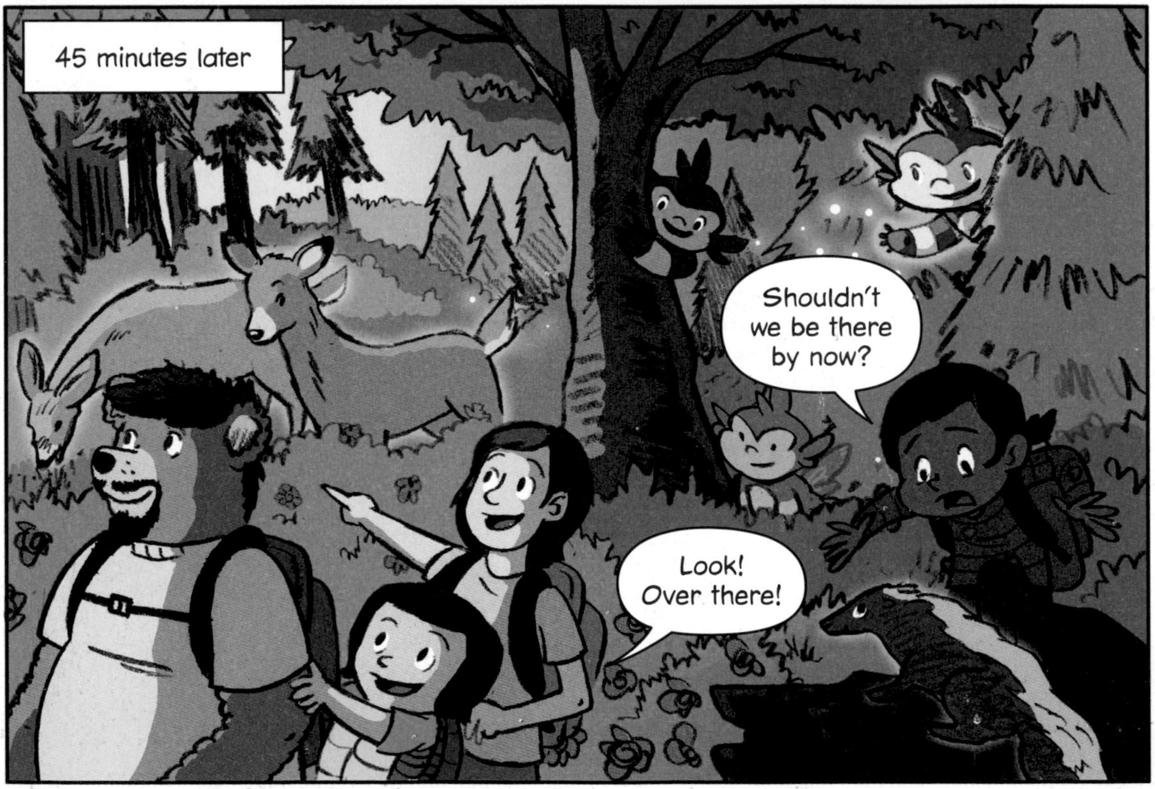
45 minutes later
Shouldn't we be there by now?
Look! Over there!

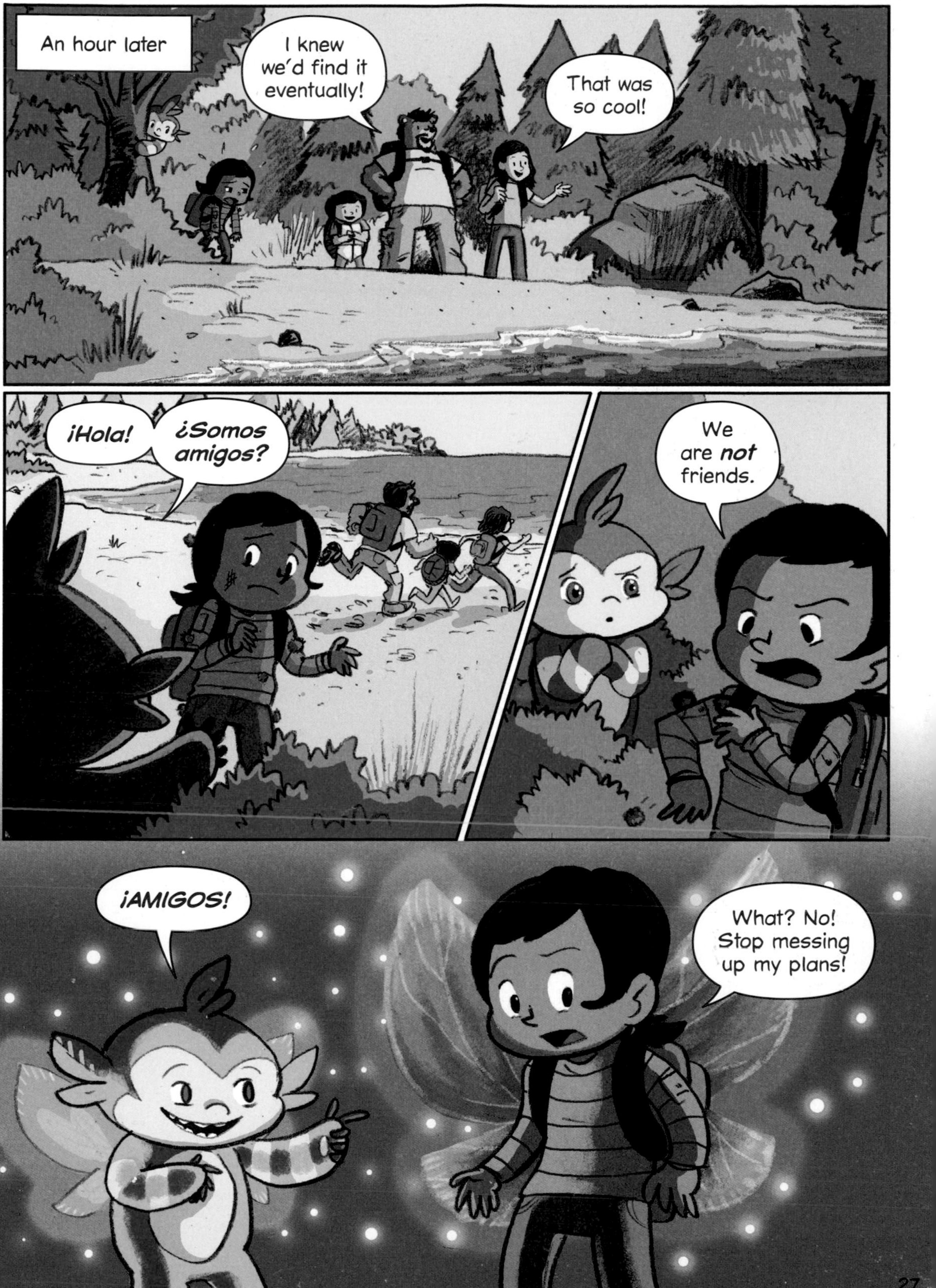
An hour later
I knew we'd find it eventually!
That was so cool!
¡Hola!
¿Somos amigos?
We are *not* friends.
¡AMIGOS!
What? No! Stop messing up my plans!

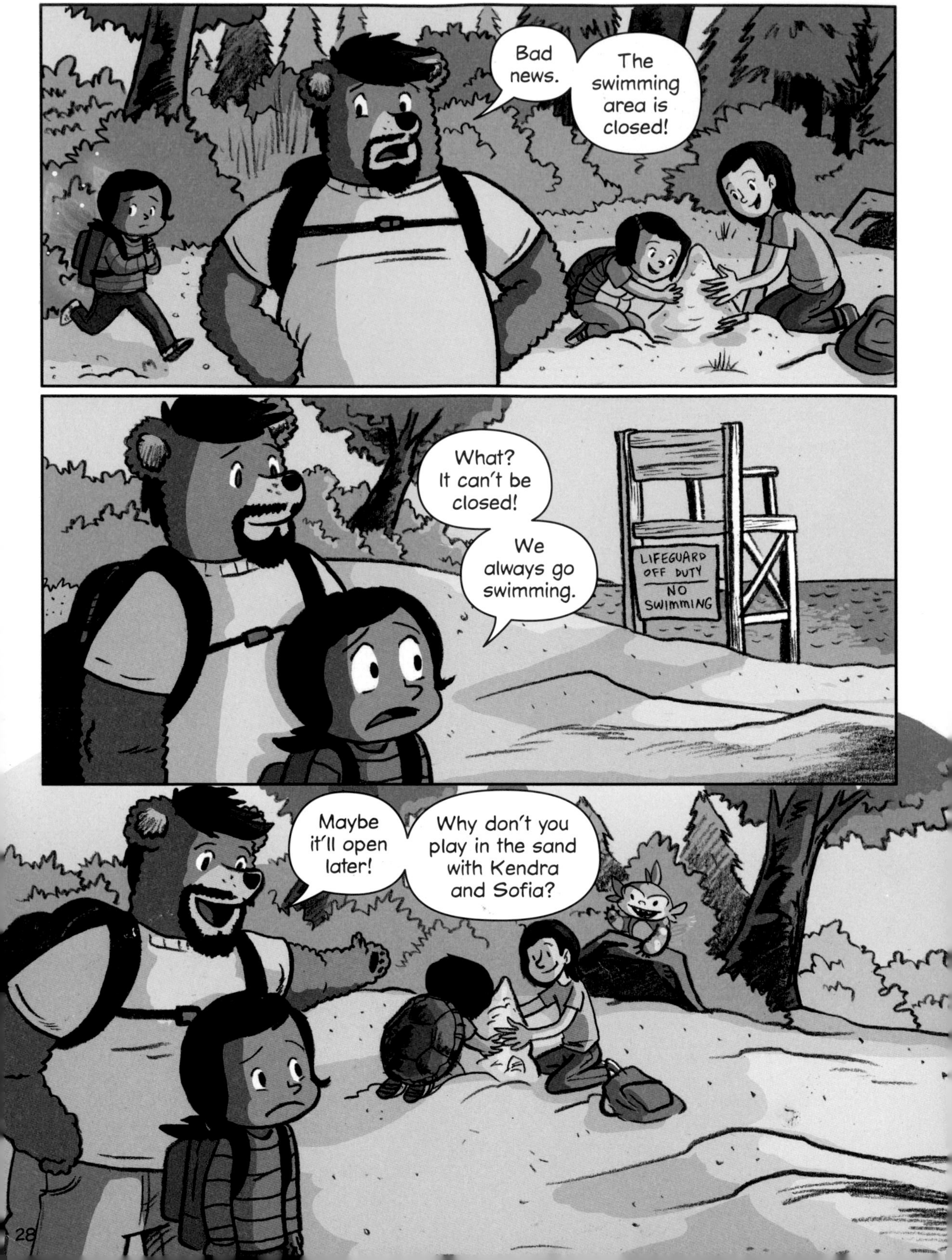
Bad news.
The swimming area is closed!
What? It can't be closed!
We always go swimming.
LIFEGUARD OFF DUTY
NO SWIMMING
Maybe it'll open later!
Why don't you play in the sand with Kendra and Sofia?

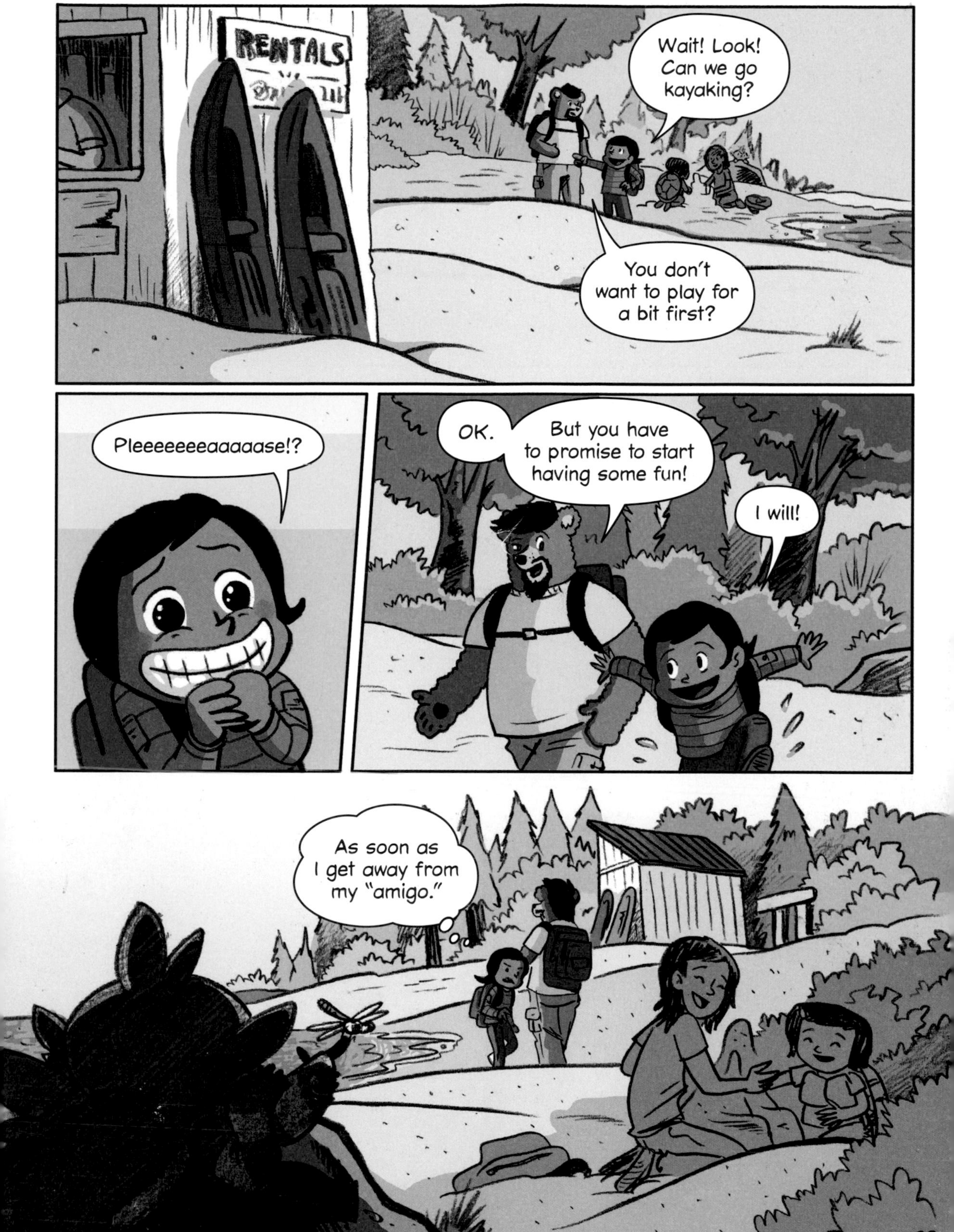

RENTALS
Wait! Look! Can we go kayaking?
You don't want to play for a bit first?
Pleeeeeeeaaaaase!?
OK.
But you have to promise to start having some fun!
I will!
As soon as I get away from my "amigo."

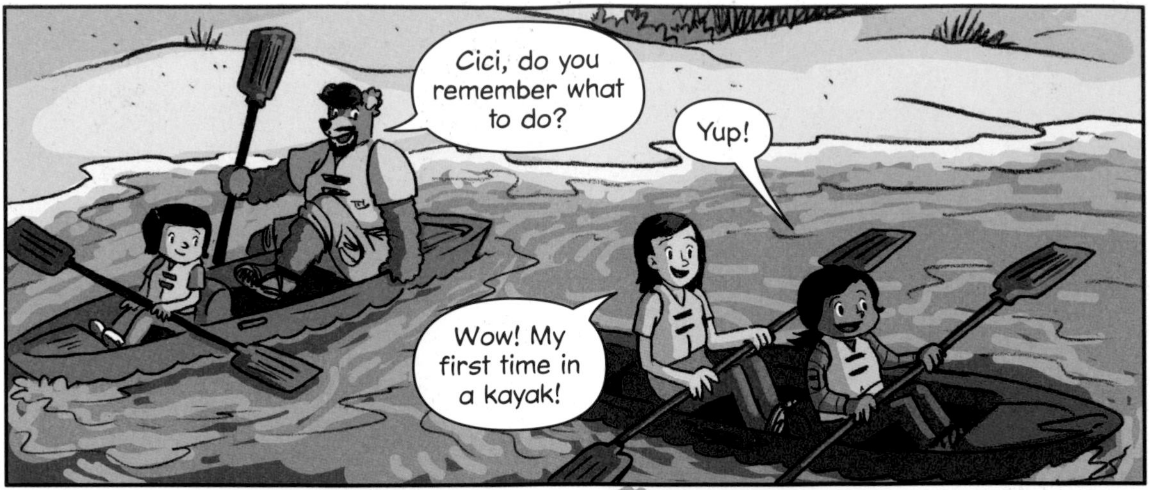
Cici, do you remember what to do?
Yup!
Wow! My first time in a kayak!

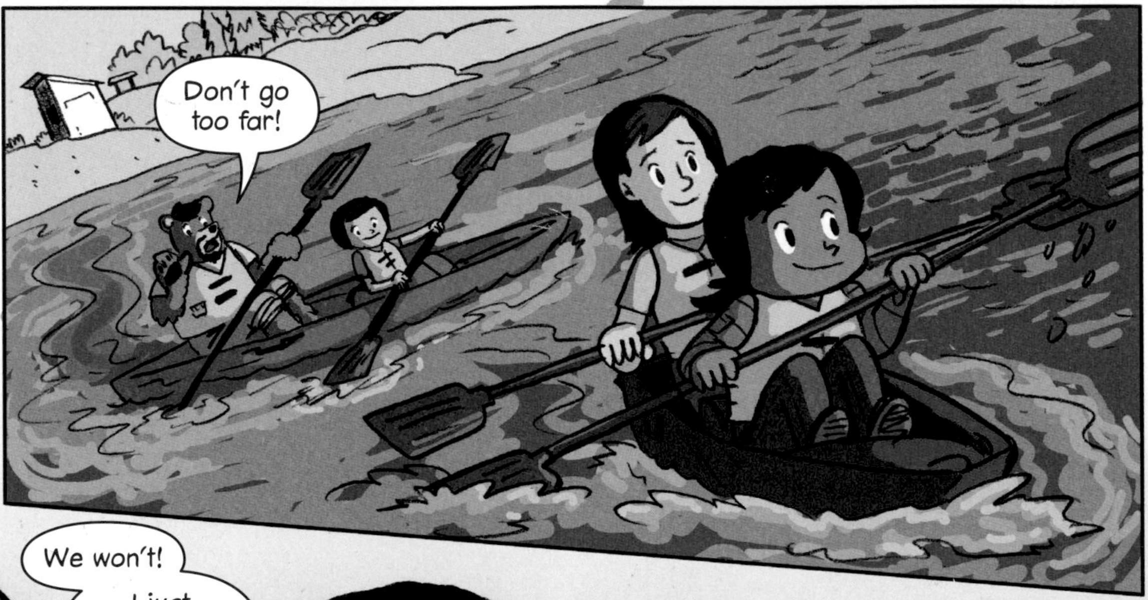
Don't go too far!

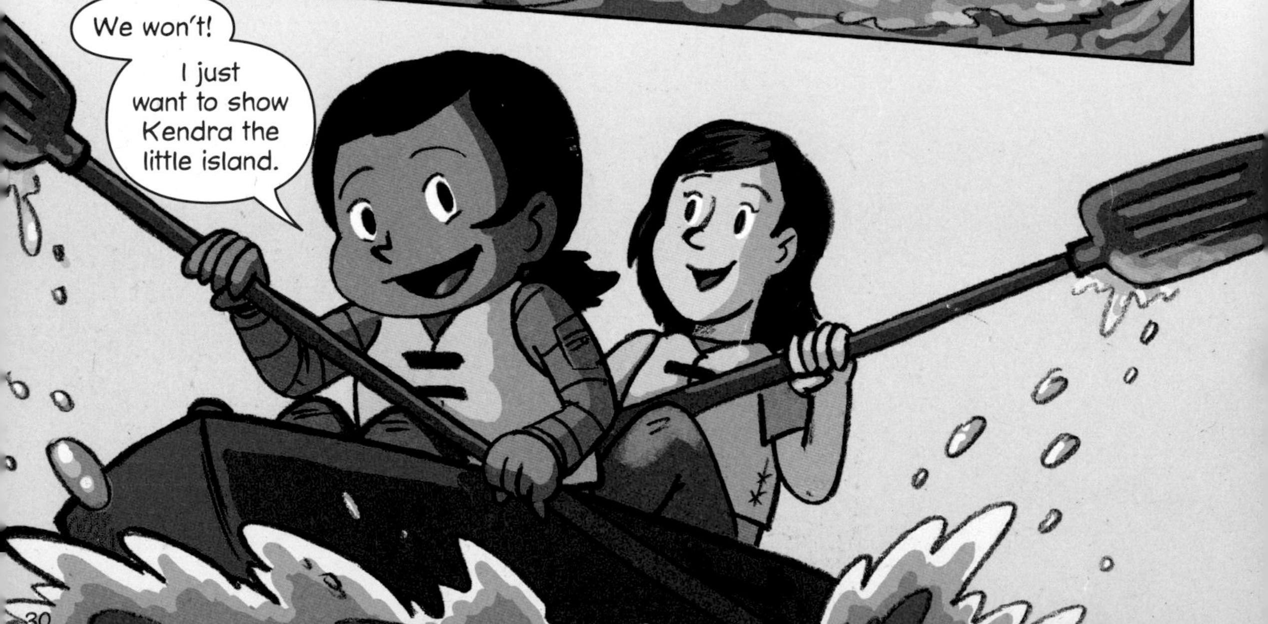
We won't!
I just want to show Kendra the little island.

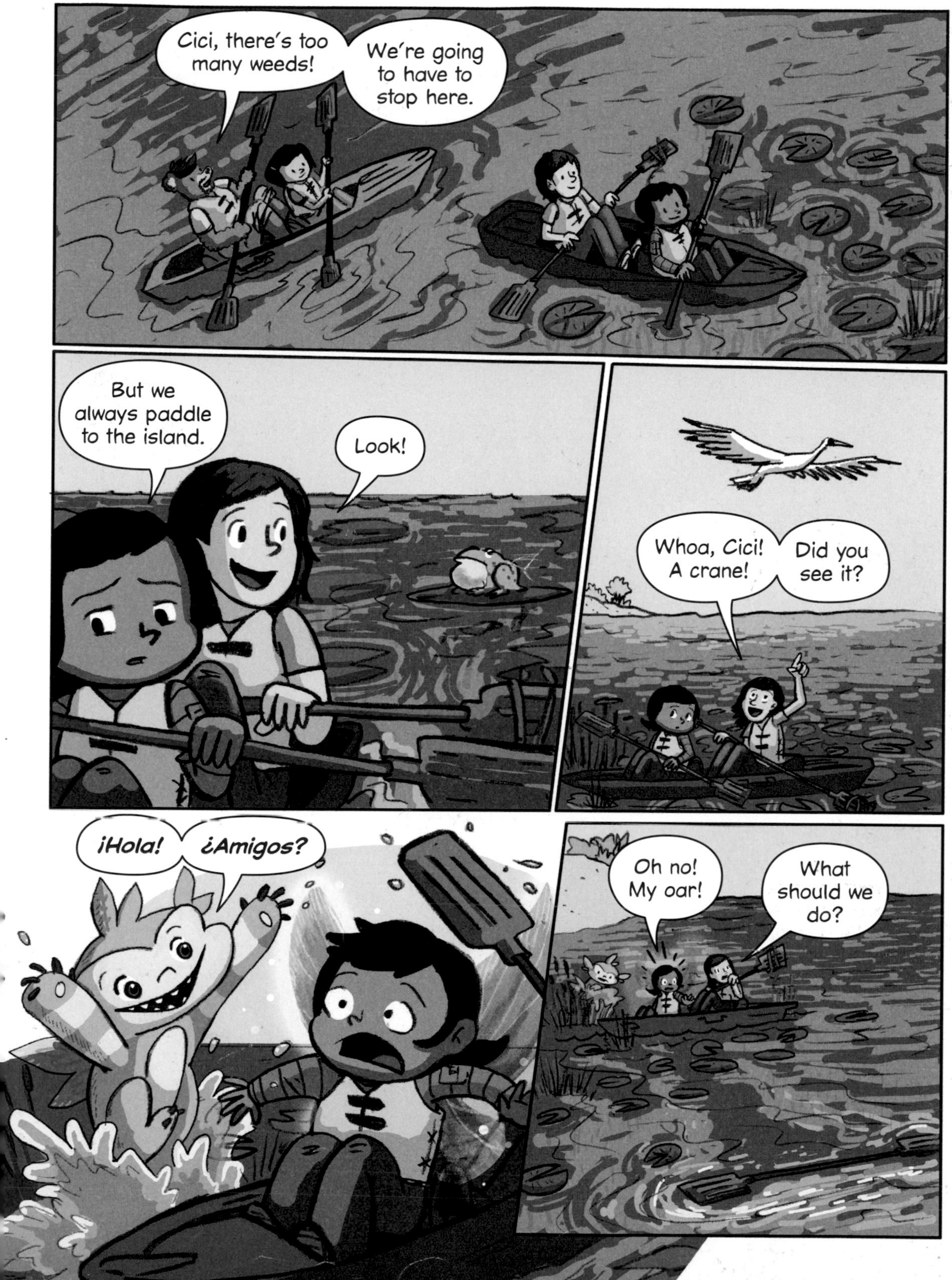
Cici, there's too many weeds!
We're going to have to stop here.
But we always paddle to the island.
Look!
Whoa, Cici! A crane!
Did you see it?
¡Hola!
¿Amigos?
Oh no! My oar!
What should we do?

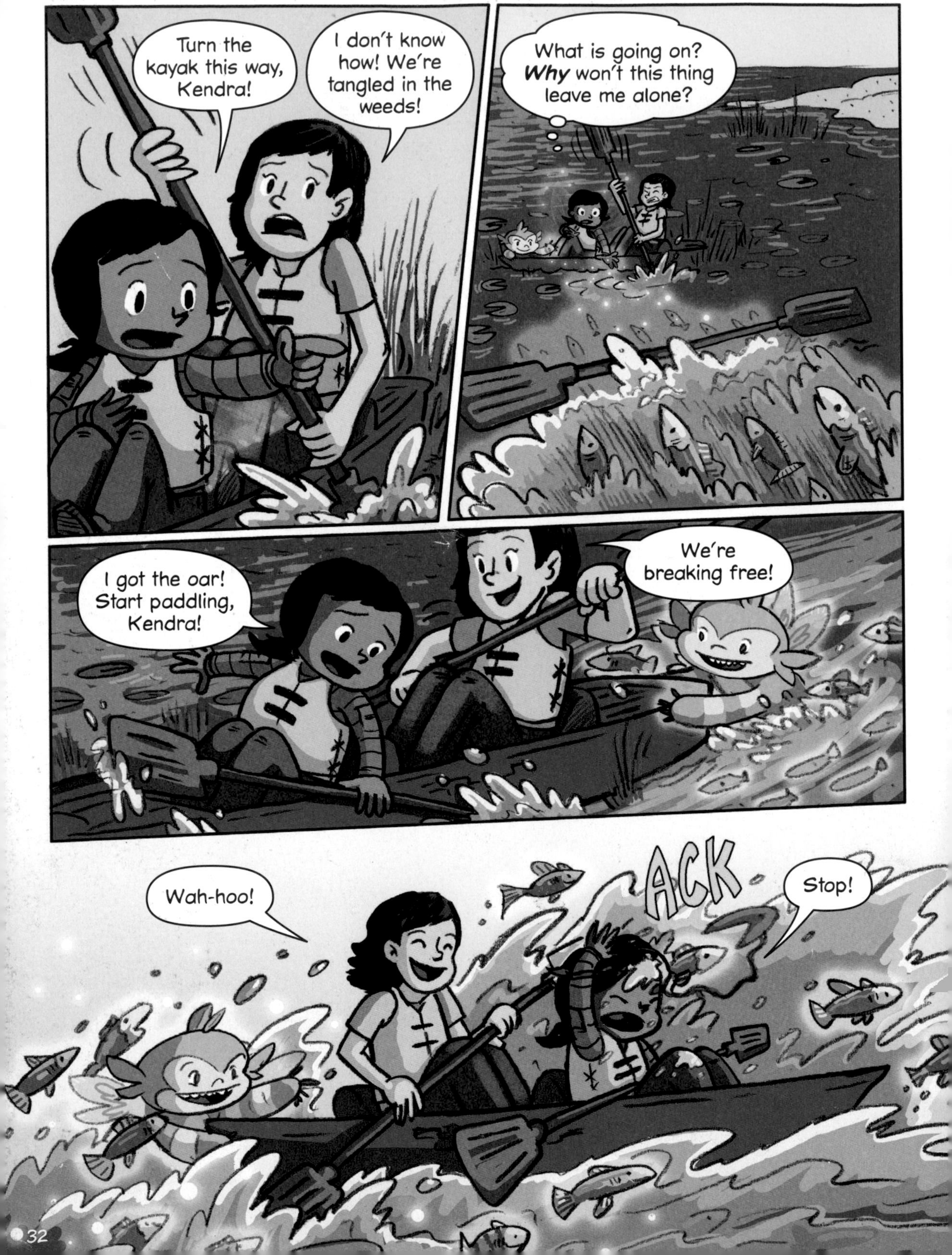
Turn the kayak this way, Kendra!
I don't know how! We're tangled in the weeds!
What is going on? *Why* won't this thing leave me alone?
I got the oar! Start paddling, Kendra!
We're breaking free!
Wah-hoo!
ACK
Stop!

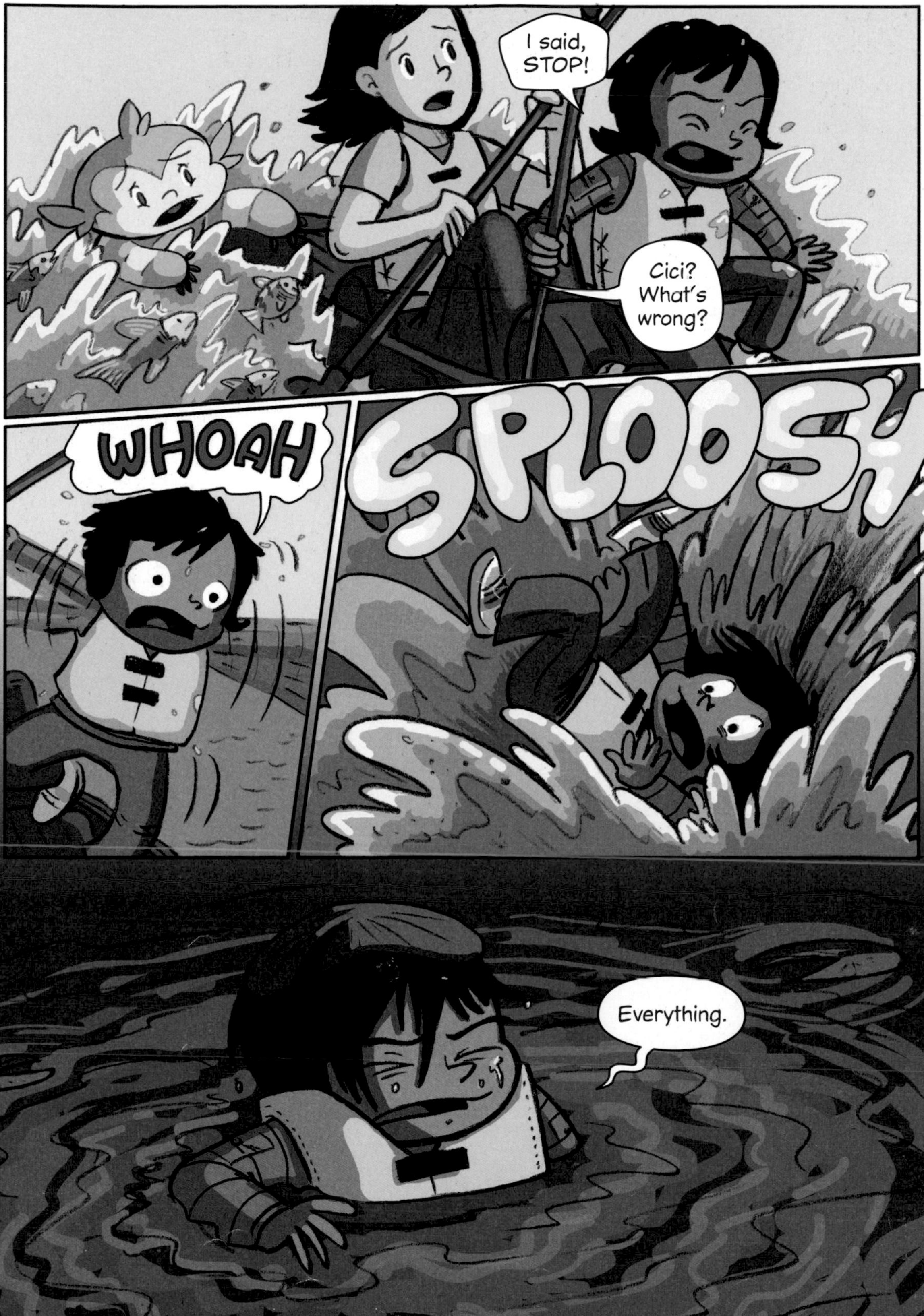
I said, STOP!
Cici? What's wrong?
WHOAH
SPLOOSH
Everything.

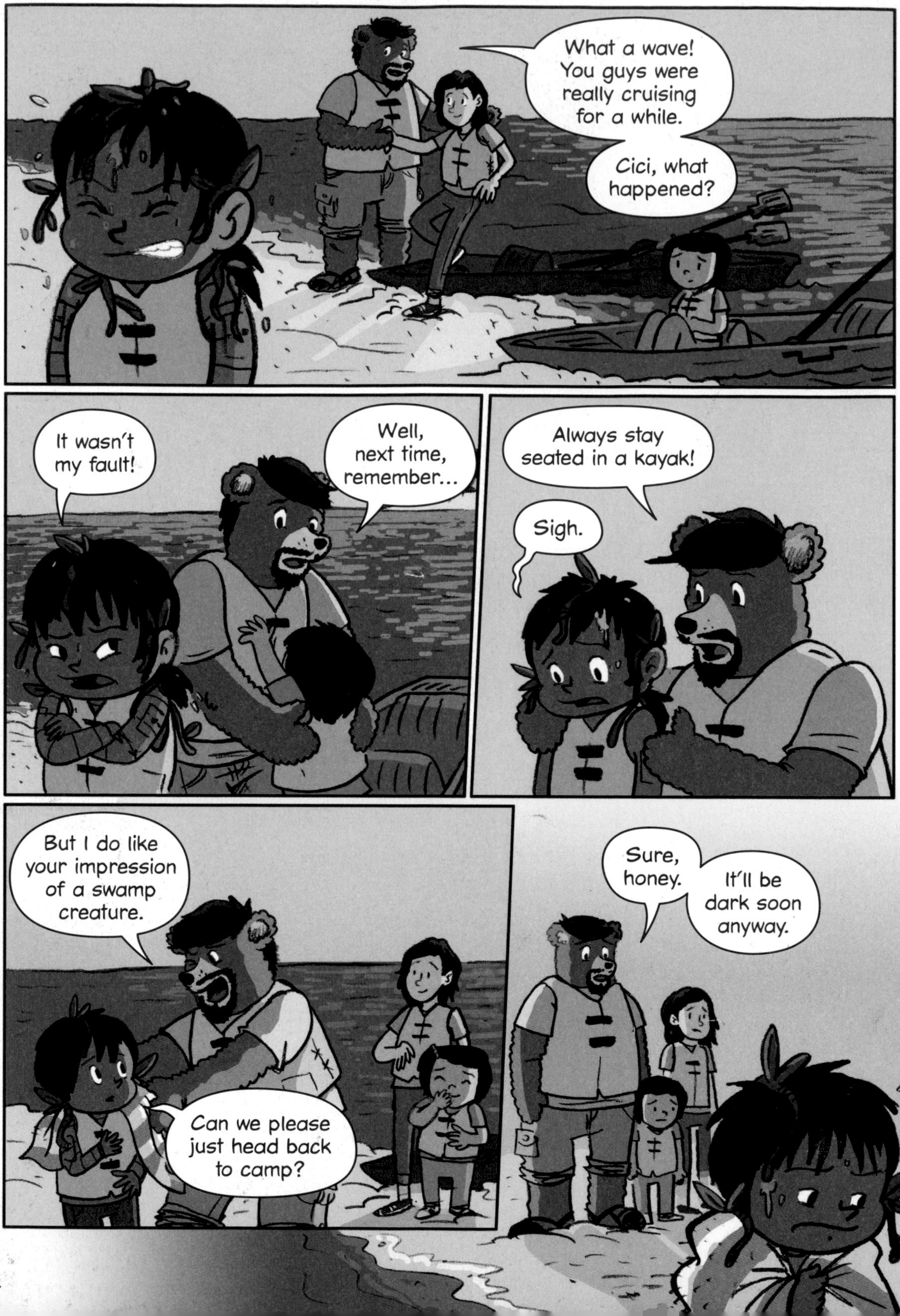
What a wave! You guys were really cruising for a while.
Cici, what happened?
It wasn't my fault!
Well, next time, remember...
Always stay seated in a kayak!
Sigh.
But I do like your impression of a swamp creature.
Can we please just head back to camp?
Sure, honey.
It'll be dark soon anyway.

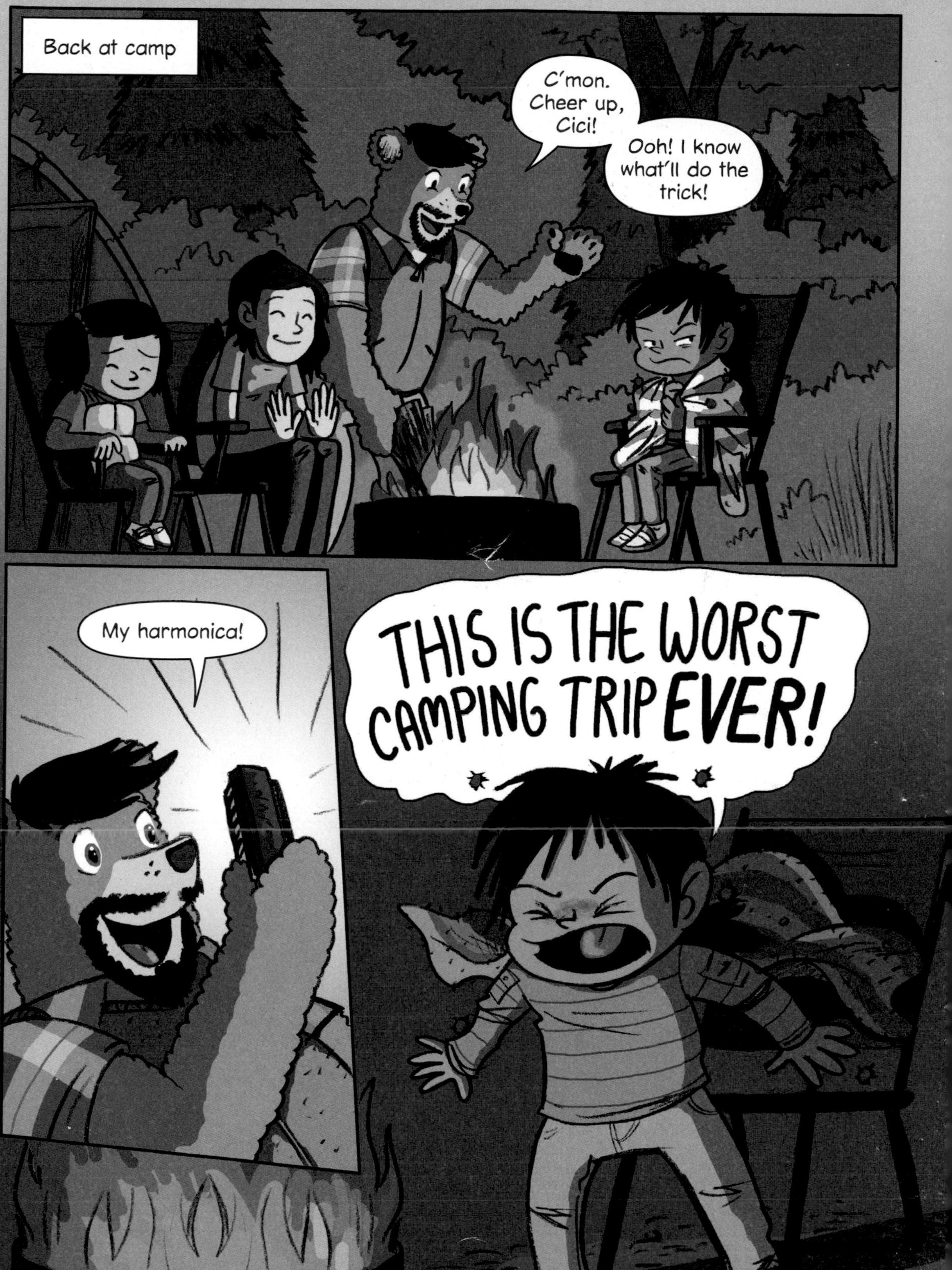
Back at camp
C'mon. Cheer up, Cici!
Ooh! I know what'll do the trick!
My harmonica!
THIS IS THE WORST CAMPING TRIP EVER!

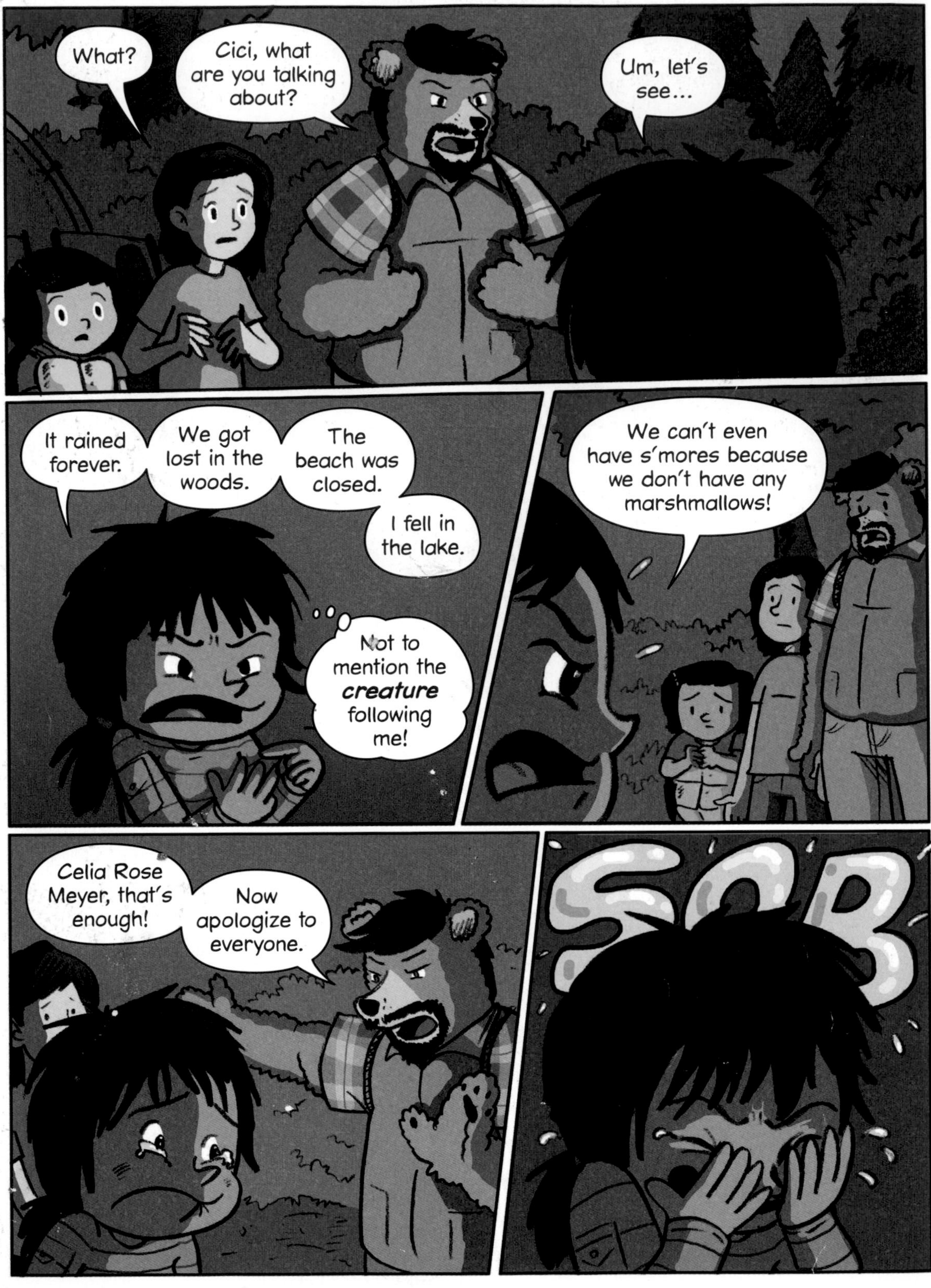
What?
Cici, what are you talking about?
Um, let's see...
It rained forever.
We got lost in the woods.
The beach was closed.
I fell in the lake.
Not to mention the ***creature*** following me!
We can't even have s'mores because we don't have any marshmallows!
Celia Rose Meyer, that's enough!
Now apologize to everyone.
SOB

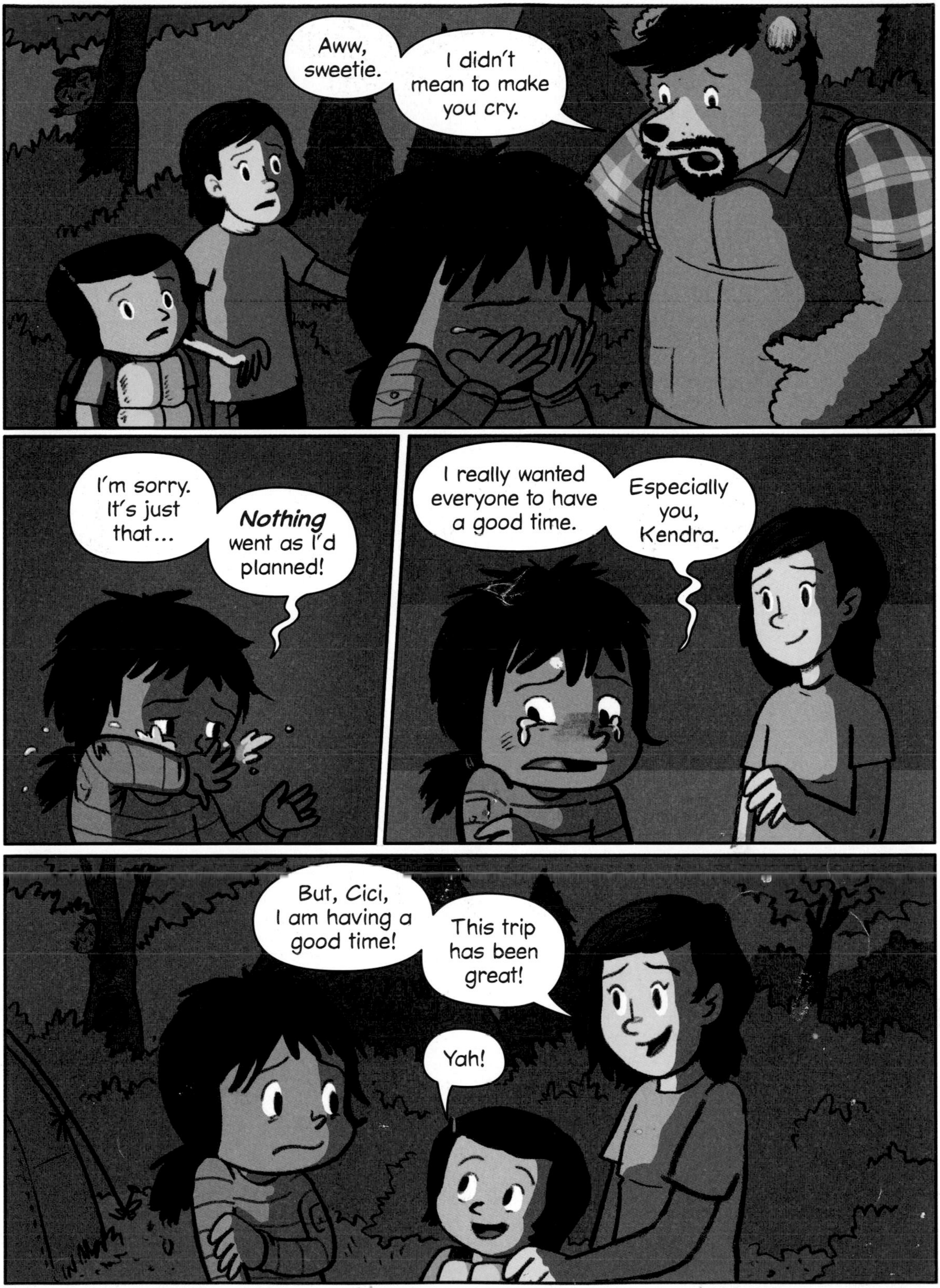
Aww, sweetie.
I didn't mean to make you cry.
I'm sorry. It's just that...
Nothing went as I'd planned!
I really wanted everyone to have a good time.
Especially you, Kendra.
But, Cici, I am having a good time!
This trip has been great!
Yah!

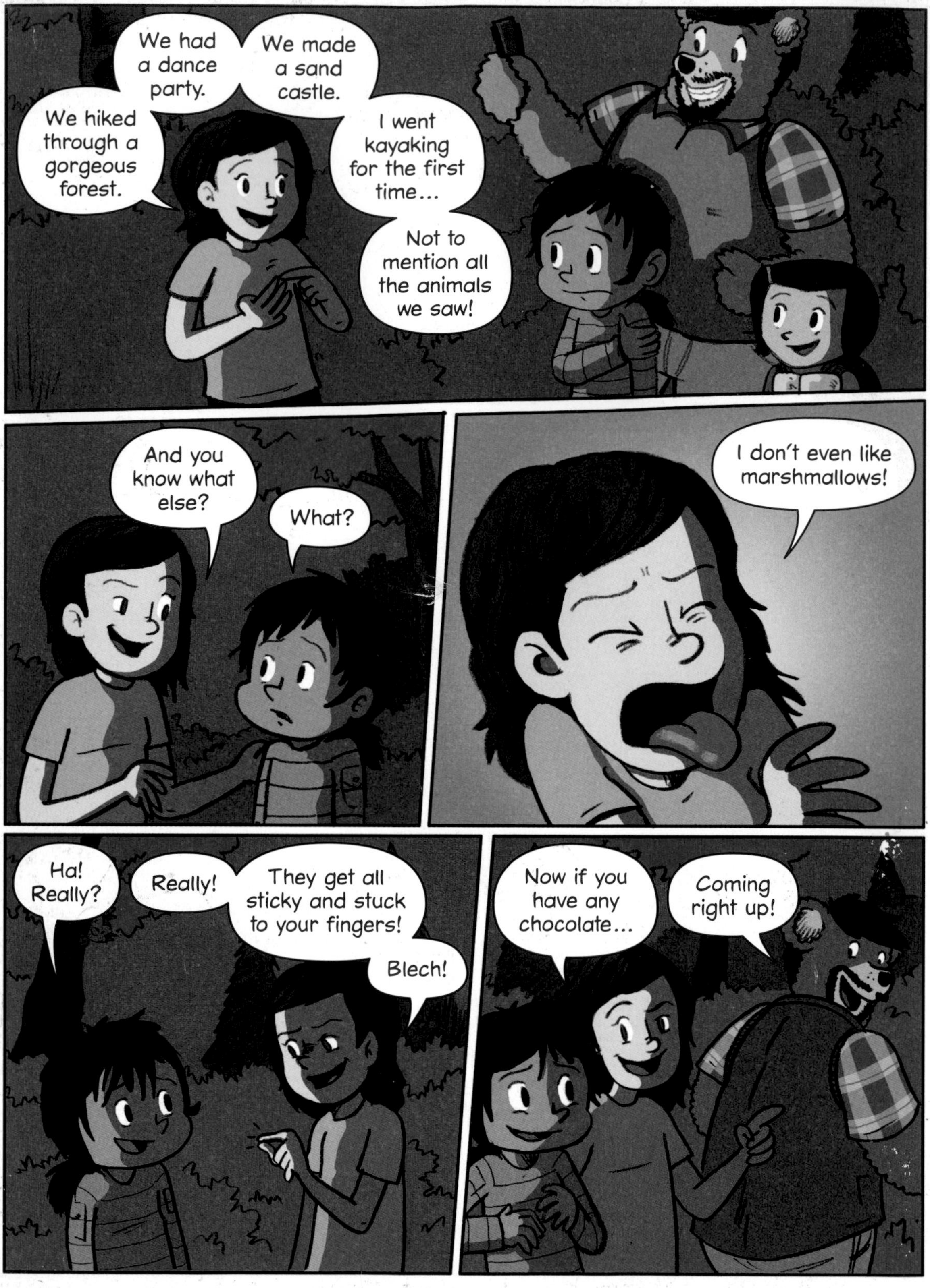
We hiked through a gorgeous forest.
We had a dance party.
We made a sand castle.
I went kayaking for the first time...
Not to mention all the animals we saw!
And you know what else?
What?
I don't even like marshmallows!
Ha! Really?
Really!
They get all sticky and stuck to your fingers!
Blech!
Now if you have any chocolate...
Coming right up!

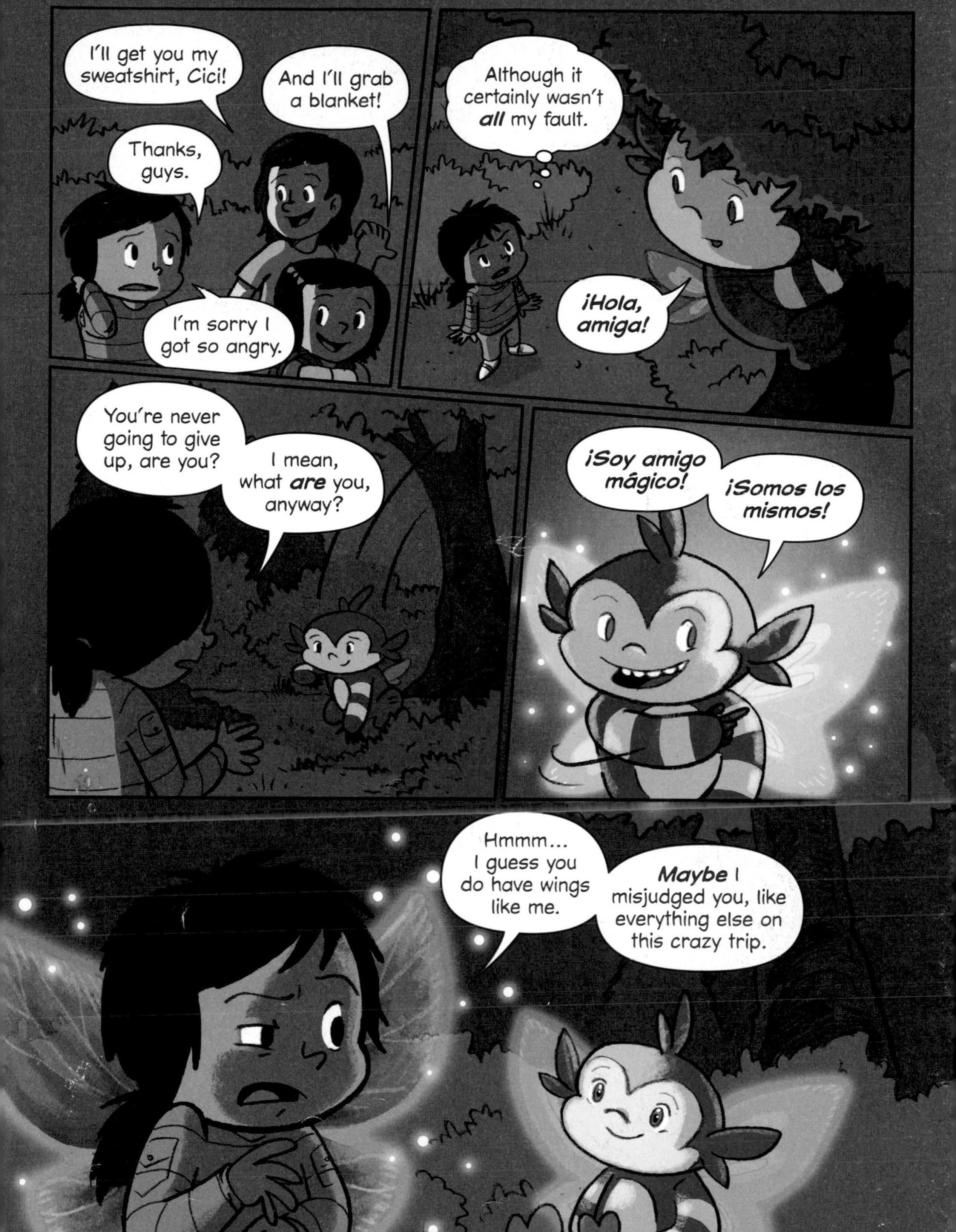
I'll get you my sweatshirt, Cici!
And I'll grab a blanket!
Thanks, guys.
I'm sorry I got so angry.
Although it certainly wasn't *all* my fault.
¡Hola, amiga!
You're never going to give up, are you?
I mean, what *are* you, anyway?
¡Soy amigo mágico!
¡Somos los mismos!
Hmmm… I guess you do have wings like me.
Maybe I misjudged you, like everything else on this crazy trip.

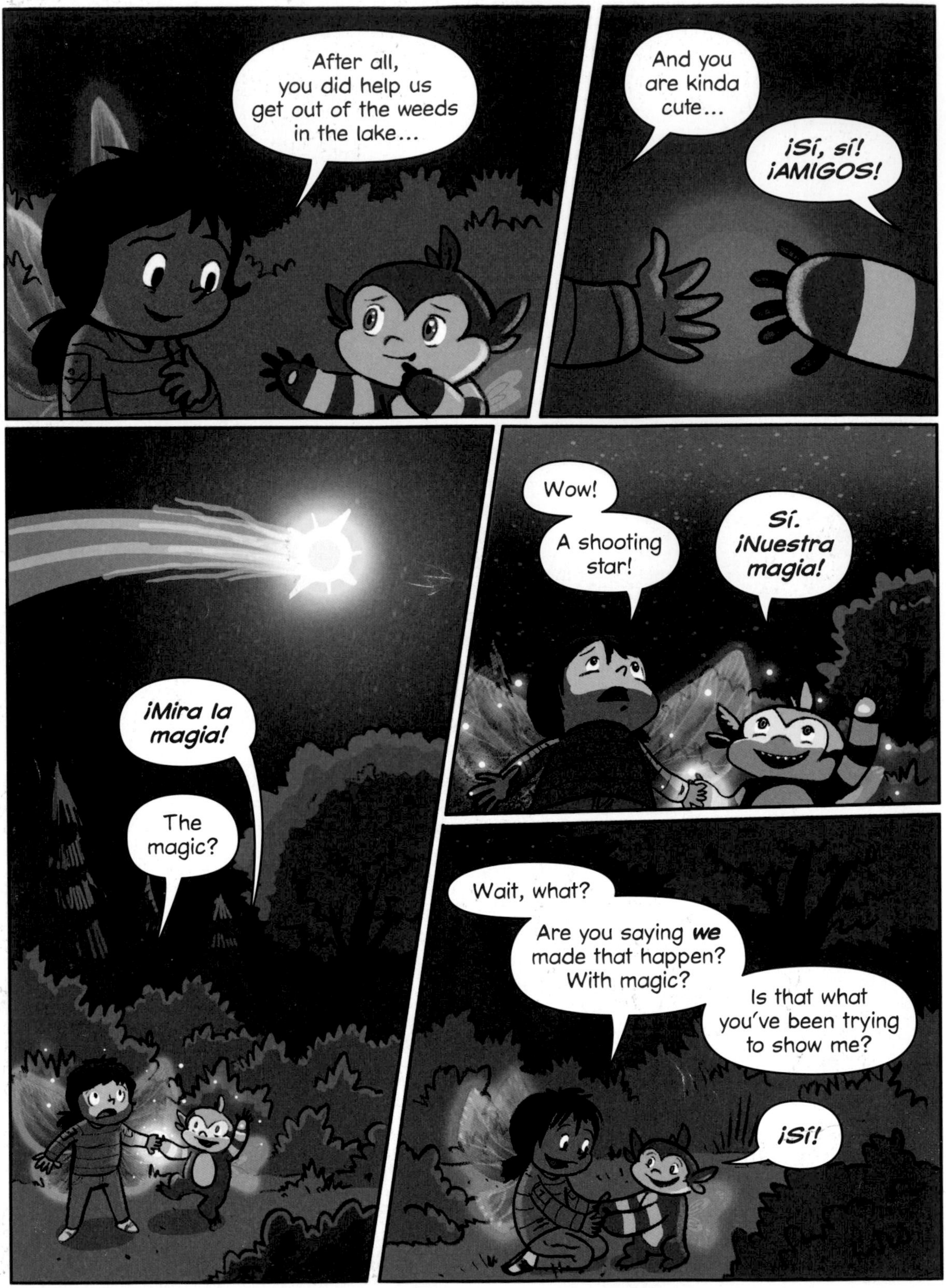
After all, you did help us get out of the weeds in the lake...
And you are kinda cute...
¡Sí, sí! ¡AMIGOS!
¡Mira la magia!
The magic?
Wow!
A shooting star!
Sí. ¡Nuestra magia!
Wait, what?
Are you saying we made that happen? With magic?
Is that what you've been trying to show me?
¡Sí!

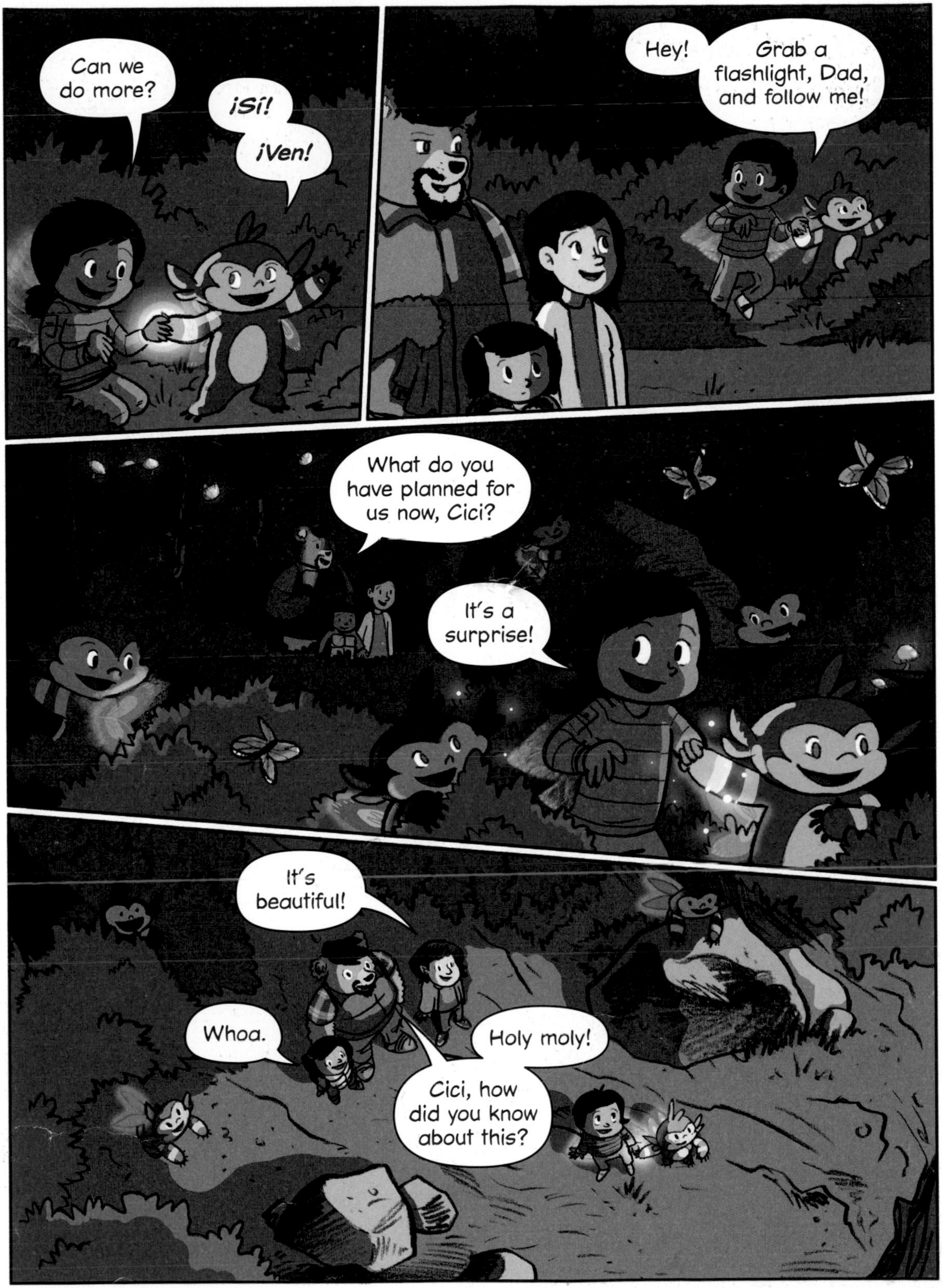
Can we do more?
¡Sí!
¡Ven!
Hey!
Grab a flashlight, Dad, and follow me!
What do you have planned for us now, Cici?
It's a surprise!
It's beautiful!
Whoa.
Holy moly!
Cici, how did you know about this?

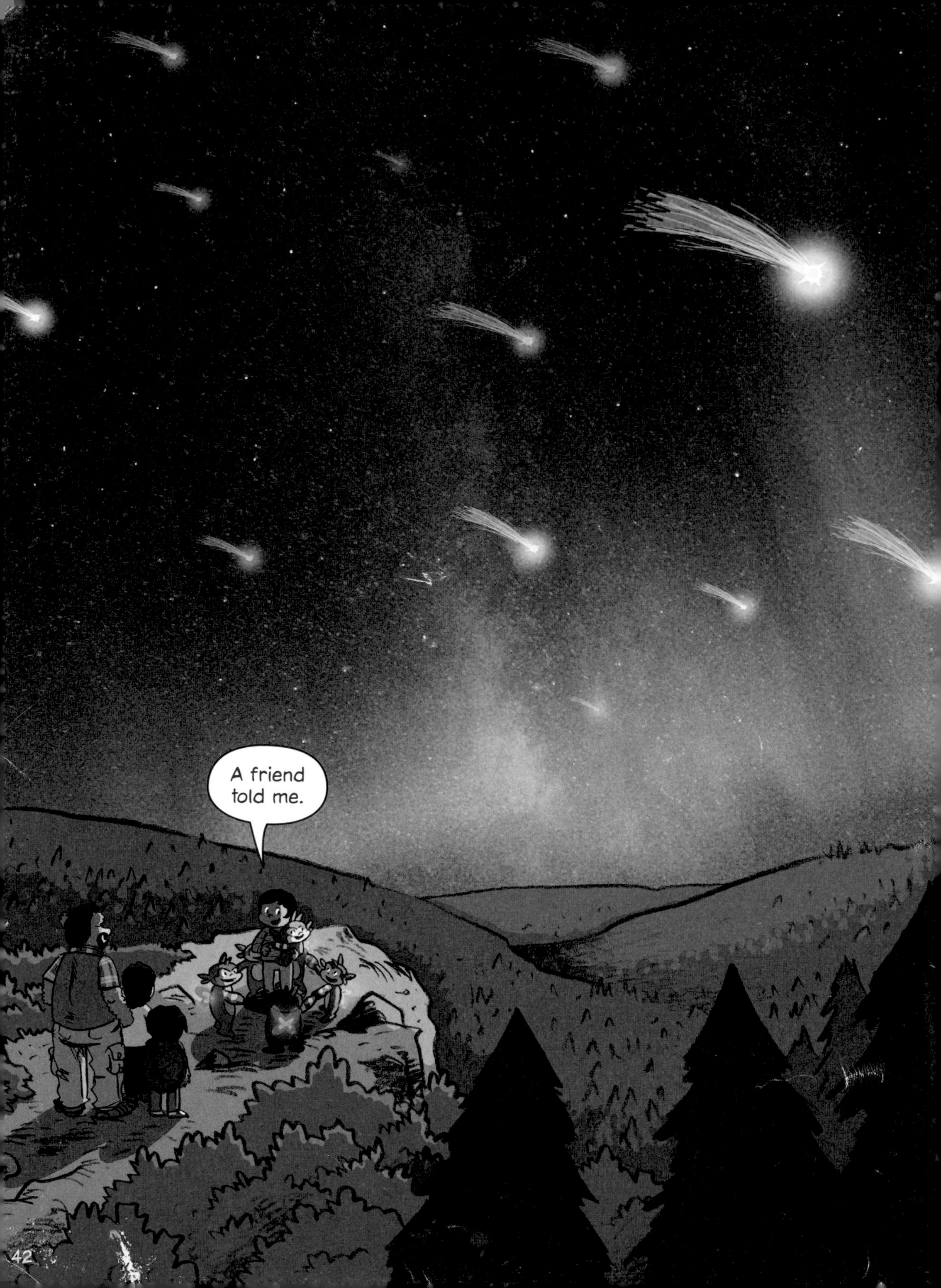
A friend told me.

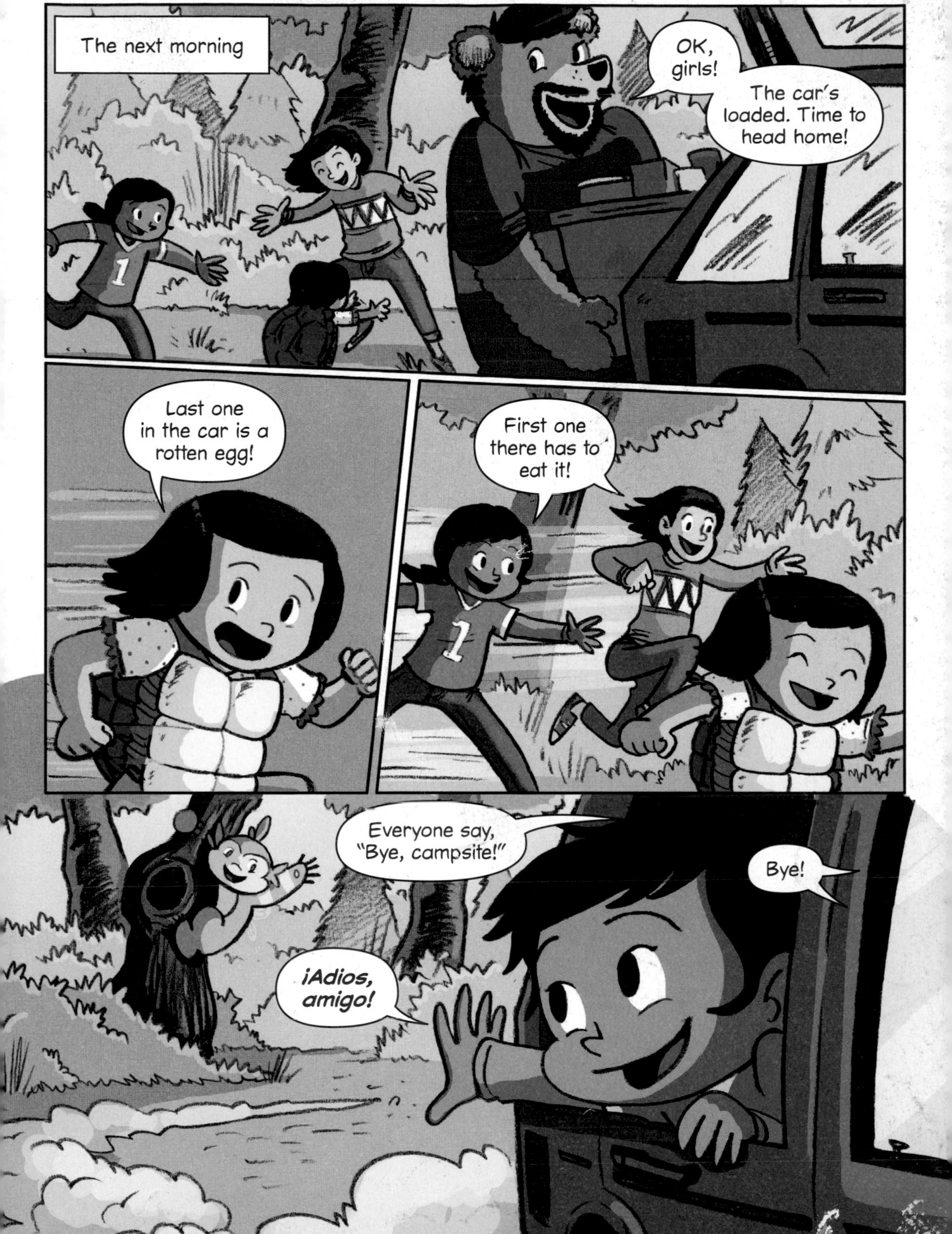
The next morning
OK, girls!
The car's loaded. Time to head home!
Last one in the car is a rotten egg!
First one there has to eat it!
Everyone say, "Bye, campsite!"
Bye!
¡Adios, amigo!

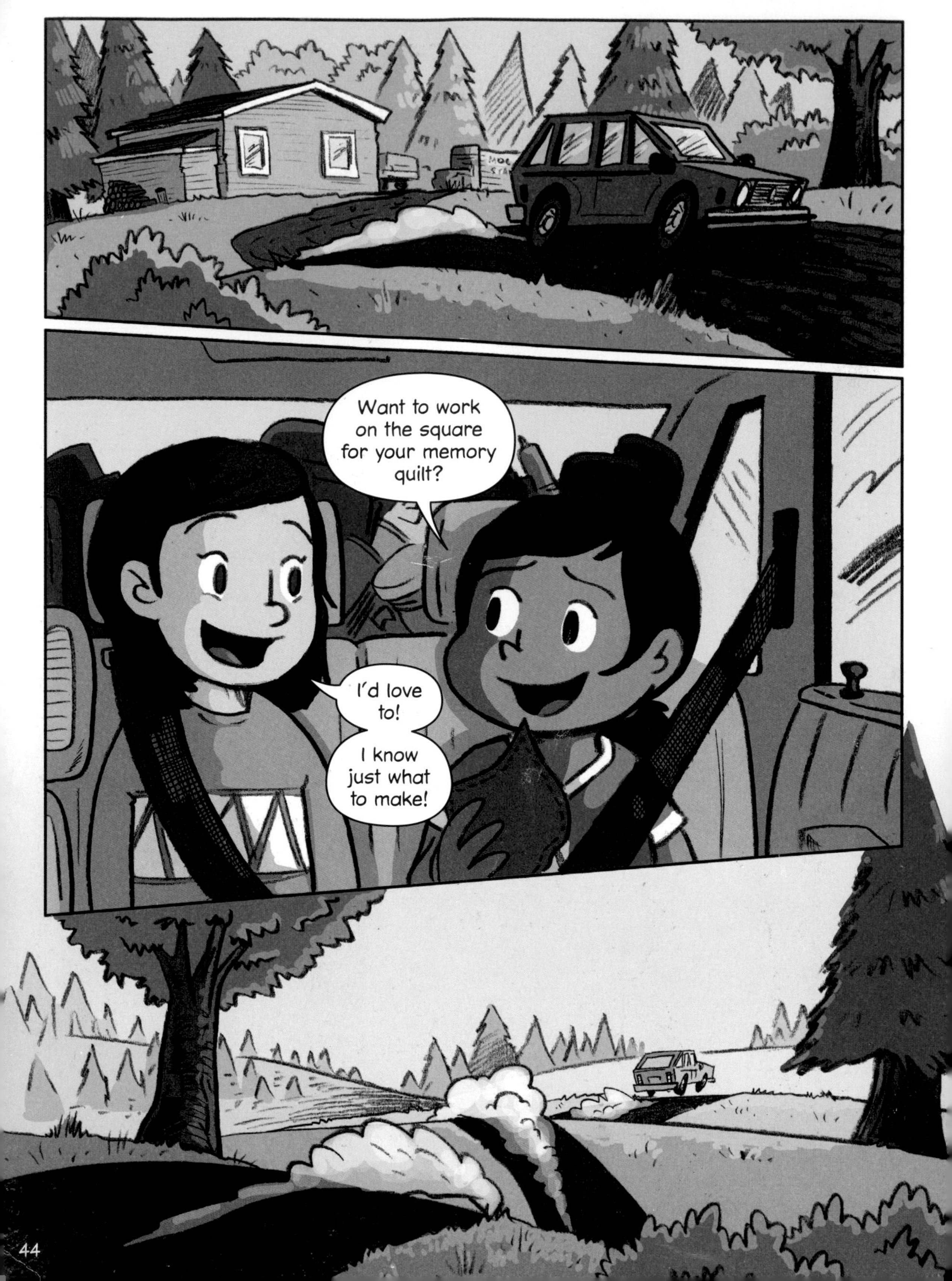
Want to work on the square for your memory quilt?
I'd love to!
I know just what to make!

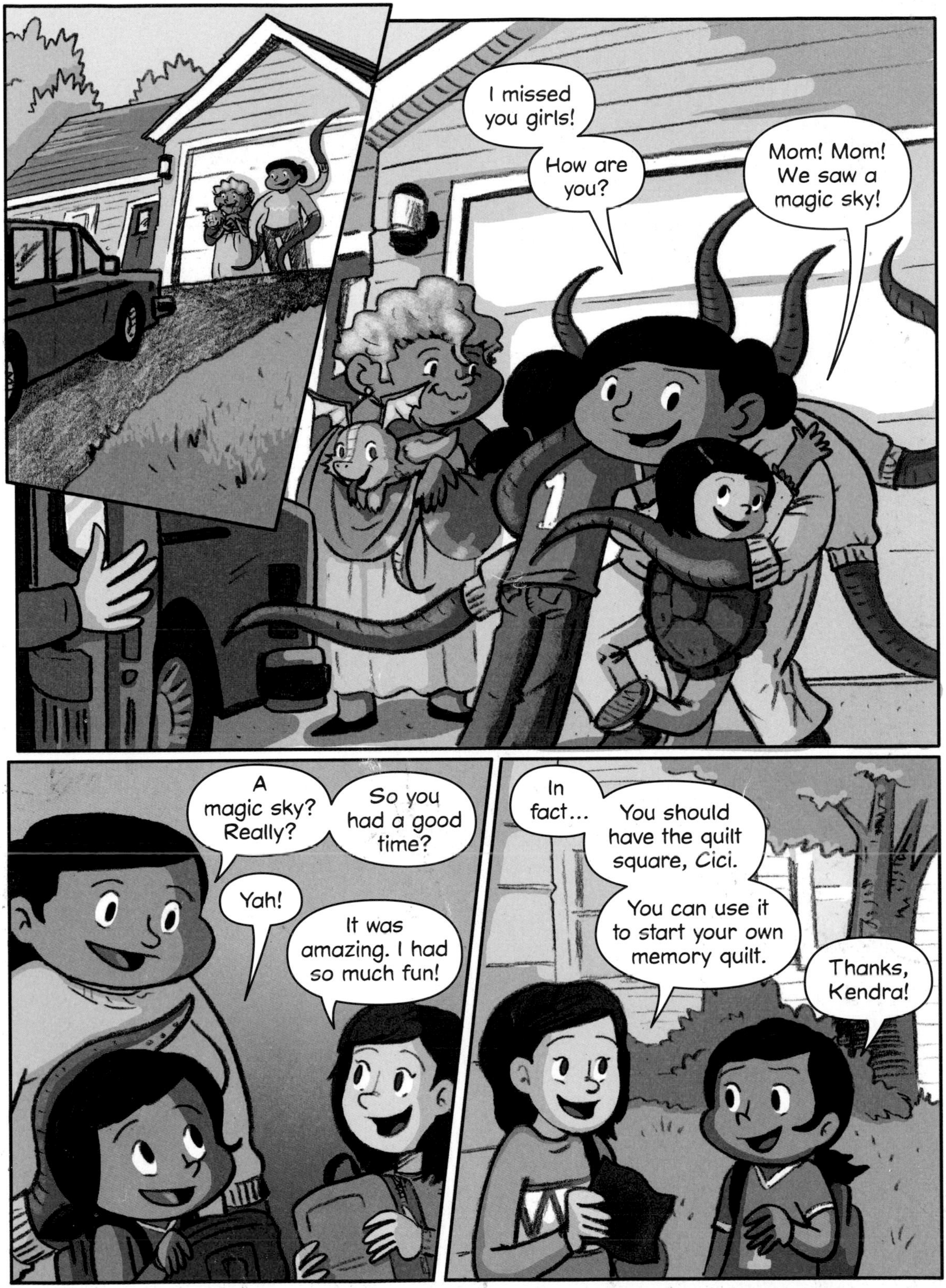
I missed you girls!
How are you?
Mom! Mom! We saw a magic sky!
A magic sky? Really?
So you had a good time?
Yah!
It was amazing. I had so much fun!
In fact...
You should have the quilt square, Cici.
You can use it to start your own memory quilt.
Thanks, Kendra!

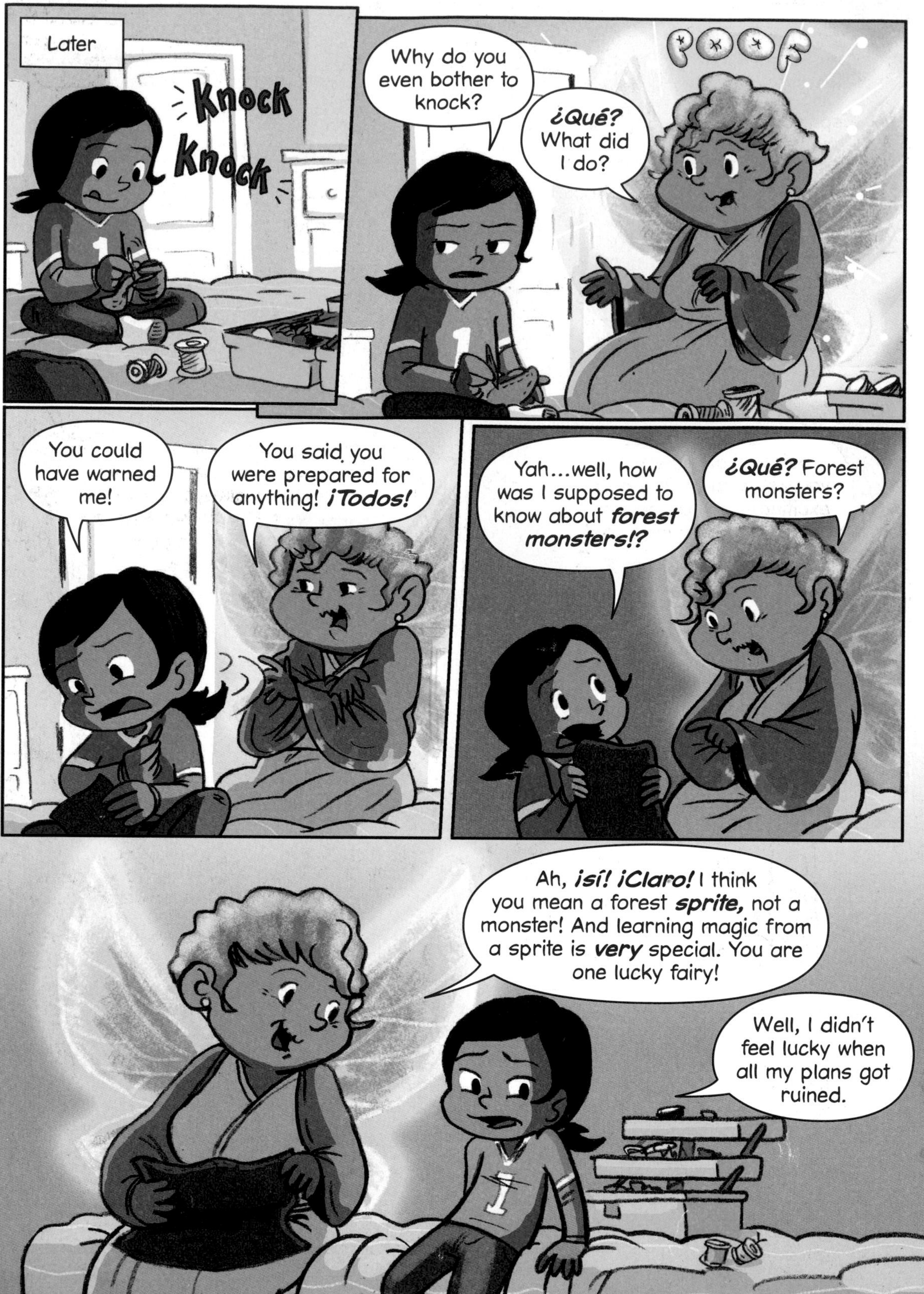
Later
Knock Knock
Why do you even bother to knock?
POOF
¿Qué? What did I do?
You could have warned me!
You said you were prepared for anything! ¡Todos!
Yah...well, how was I supposed to know about forest monsters!?
¿Qué? Forest monsters?
Ah, ¡sí! ¡Claro! I think you mean a forest sprite, not a monster! And learning magic from a sprite is very special. You are one lucky fairy!
Well, I didn't feel lucky when all my plans got ruined.

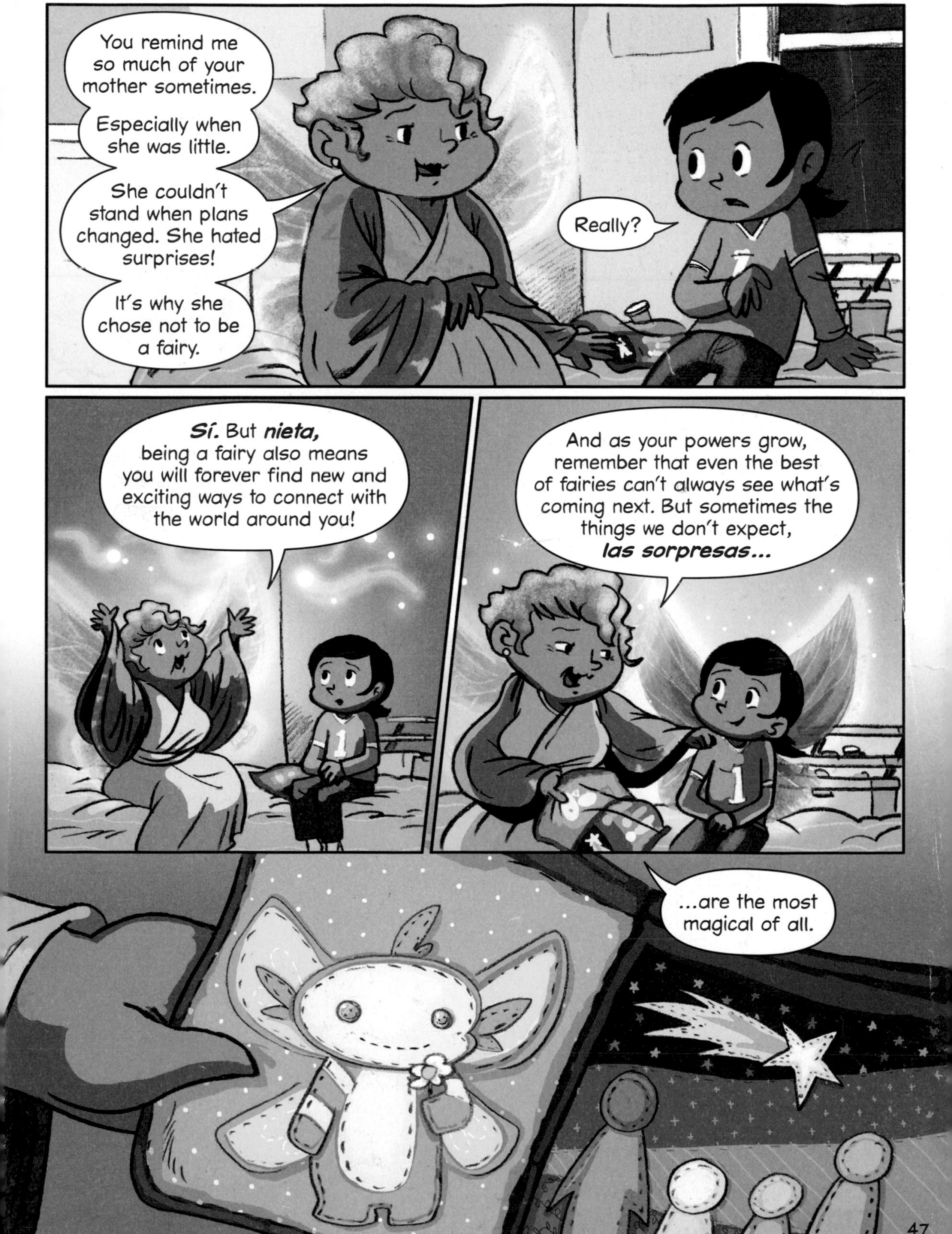

You remind me so much of your mother sometimes.
Especially when she was little.
She couldn't stand when plans changed. She hated surprises!
It's why she chose not to be a fairy.
Really?
Sí. But *nieta,* being a fairy also means you will forever find new and exciting ways to connect with the world around you!
And as your powers grow, remember that even the best of fairies can't always see what's coming next. But sometimes the things we don't expect, *las sorpresas...*
...are the most magical of all.

About the Author and Illustrator

Cori Doerrfeld is a freelance author and illustrator who holds degrees from St. Olaf College and the Minneapolis College of Art and Design. She has written and illustrated several picture books, including *Penny Loves Pink*, *Little Bunny Foo Foo: The Real Story*, *Matilda in the Middle*, and *Maggie and Wendel*. She lives in Minneapolis with her comic artist husband, Tyler Page, and their two children, Charlotte and Leo. You can follow Cori's work on her website: www.coridoerrfeld.com.

Tyler Page is an Eisner-nominated and Xeric Grant–winning artist and educator. In addition to publishing his own work, he illustrated the Graphic Universe series Chicagoland Detective Agency and has created comics and illustrations for a variety of commercial clients. He is also the director of Print Technology Services at the Minneapolis College of Art and Design. He lives in Minneapolis with his wife, author/illustrator Cori Doerrfeld, and their two children.